♦ ♦ ♦

Welcome to Stories for Short Journeys. short stories which have no theme, except that they are probably long enough to read while you wait for something. A dentist appointment, your commute to work, while you drink a cup of tea or wait for a phone call? Whatever it is. We are all so busy now, and we live so fast, taking a break to jump into another world is a treat.

I hope that you enjoy these stories. They are random and some are a little off the wall. Life is like that sometimes. I think of short stories as snippets of conversation that you hear as you go about your day, and a novel as a long conversation, over dinner, with a good glass of wine. However you found your way here, I am so glad that you did.

If you enjoy the last story, then you may want to look out for a new collection of short stories, coming soon which does have a theme. The last story in this book, is the first story in the next. A taster, perhaps.

I want to thank my family who have been hugely supportive of my writing, and have forgiven my distraction for so long, perhaps they have forgotten how life was when I was paying attention.

1.

A Good Cup of Coffee

Don't ever underestimate her. She's super smart. I know that's what they say. She gave tax advice to people who had laundered very dirty money and still had no wish to fill the revenue's coffers. She may look like she's not paying attention, but she will take it all in. I hear them talking. I hear them saying it.

The room is comfortable enough. I have lived in a good deal worse. They want me to tell them who I worked for. What I advised. As if I would tell them, it would be madness to open my mouth, even to ask for a cup of coffee. Oh, I miss decent coffee. I miss it so much. I miss hairdressers. My hair has grown out, the expensive highlights gone, replaced by mousy brown.

Two suits arrive to see me most weeks, on a Wednesday. Perhaps that's their slow day.

"Hello Moira." They say, all smiles and sweetness. "We brought you in a cup of coffee." I take the hot cup and sniff. The smell is heaven. "We need to ask you some questions." I nod. "About your clients, the people you advised." I nod again. "Can you tell us their names? How they contacted you?"

"I don't remember." I smile. They know I do.

"Moira. You're sitting in here. Is it fair that they are free to get on with their lives and you are here?" He smiles as though he is on my side. He wants to be my friend.

"I wish I could help you. Why am I here? No charge, no trial, no reason to hold me." I allow myself a sip of the coffee. It fails to live up to the promise made by the aroma.

"You are being held here under special rules which govern funding of organized crime. We can, as you know, hold you indefinitely. Nobody knows where you are, nobody can get to you here." He smiles the toothpaste advert smile he thinks is cute.

"I would like to speak to a lawyer, or speak to a member of my family, or speak to anyone who does not work for the revenue." I smile sweetly. "Please."

"That won't be possible until you speak to us."

I sit back and drink my coffee. This happens once a week. Every week, it has not varied in all the time I have been here. All because I came up with the genius plan, the perfect loophole, the guaranteed no inheritance tax, no risk, minimal income tax plan, which has saved some very influential people some vast sums of money. It has legitimized some very dirty money, and kept the next generation of little thugs in a good living, without any laws being broken. It was, I have to say, absolute bloody genius.

I will refuse to tell them who I advised, that would sign my death warrant, and that of anyone I have ever cared about. I will keep my mouth shut and hug the information close to my heart. The thing is, if you have dirty money, and you want to clean it, you put it through a business where cash is expected, like a hairdressers', or a bar. You then pay tax on it, and it's clean. The trouble is, if you are a criminal, you don't want to keep on paying tax on it. You now are left with piles of clean cash which you want to leave to your children, and the government are waiting with their tongues hanging out to take forty percent of your hard-earned money.

My advice was simple. Set up a limited company, make a loan of your clean money to the company, and the company then buys property. Which is rented out. The money the company makes from the rent, is paid out in loan payments to you, at no interest, so you pay no tax on the income, and the company pays minimal tax on very low profits. After a year or so, you decide to retire from the business, and take on Directors, your children. They earn nothing from the company, and you keep on getting the loan paid back, and seven years later, that company, and as many properties as you have bought is tax free, non-declarable, the possession of your children. Simple, and easy, legal, and bloody genius.

The thing is, the government found out that this was what was happening, some idiot probably told them, and they are trying to close the loop-hole, but they can only do that if they can prove that someone set up the company with the intention to defraud the tax man. They can only do that if someone admits it, or I give them the names. So, you see how this is a deadlock. We all know that they will not get me to talk to them, any more than anyone who has a brain would admit they have taken my advice.

I miss things about being outside, but this is better than a prison, better than a lot of people live I suppose, except, there is nobody to talk to, apart from the suits. My brain whirs with ideas, my head is stuffed full of them, but I am required to keep them in, locked up tight. Mostly I miss the freedom to choose. To choose what I eat and when, and to choose good coffee and to choose how my hair looks. Little chunks of freedom that seem bigger when you have none.

The night after the suits visited, I heard a knock on the door. I had no key, I could not open it if I wanted to, but I was intrigued. I have always liked puzzles, that was how I came up with tax avoidance stuff. It was a quiet sound. I knocked back, the sound came again, I knocked again. Someone was out there, and I could communicate with them. It felt good.

"Moira?" The whisper came through the vent, beside the door.

"Who is it?" I crouched down to see if I could see through.

"You don't know me. I've been sent to get you out." I jumped back from the vent as though it had bitten me. The only people who would want to get me out were my ex-clients and they would only want me out because they wanted me dead, to make sure I could not tell anyone anything.

"I've said nothing, and I won't. Go away." I pushed myself as far as I could to the other side of the room.

"Moira. I'm being paid a great deal of money to get you out. Nobody is going to hurt you if that's what you're worried about." I heard the sound of something scraping in the lock.

"No. I won't go." The door pushed open, and he stood in the doorway. Judging by the size of him I would have no choice.

He put his hand around my arm and pulled. We were out and down the corridor before I had fully realized what was happening. He had disabled two guards, and the cameras would show him in a ski mask, pulling me along in his wake. My mind worked hard. If they wanted me dead, he could have just killed me there and gone. There was no reason to take me away. Unless, of course, he was not working my ex-clients, but for the suits, in the hope that I would tell him something I would not tell them. My feet were struggling to keep up with him. He was half carrying me as we left the building, and crossed the grass to a waiting van.

The doors slammed shut behind me and I was in darkness. The van moved away and I sat, waiting for my fate to become my reality. When the doors opened, I was in a large garage, and ski mask man was waiting for me to get out.

He walked away from me, and came back with a suitcase and a set of keys. He loaded the suitcase into the back of a small hatchback, and gave me the keys. He fetched a handbag, and passed that to me.

Go. Right now. There's an address in the bag, and keys to the house. Go and stay out of the way. Change your appearance. There's a fake ID in there too.

"Why?" I ran my fingers over the keys.

"There's a gun in the handbag. I know you probably never used one, but just point and shoot if you have to, you might get lucky." He peeled off his ski mask. "You helped my dad sort out the money before he died. My sisters and me are well off because of you. We got together and decided to get you out." He looked me straight in the eye. "Our parents' generation, they don't see it that way. They know Al Capone got caught on tax evasion, and they don't want to go the same way. They will be looking for you. If I could find out where you were being held, they wouldn't be far behind."

"Thank you." I opened the door of the car, and drove out of the open garage. The sun was coming up and I was free for the first time in years. I checked the address, and drove the car towards my new home. I was smiling, really smiling, for the first time in a long while. Those little chunks of freedom were falling into place.

I spotted the Starbucks drive through on the side of the road, and pulled in, ordering the biggest coffee they had and sat in the car to drink it, savouring every moment, every drop and zingy zap of caffeine. I was nearly finished, just a few sips left, when I saw movement in my wing mirror. Just a tiny movement, that was all there was, and a pop, as though someone had burst a small balloon.

I stood on the grass verge, watching the teenager from the drive through discover my body, I felt dreadful for her. Not so much for me. It had been over fast. I had enjoyed my coffee. I sipped from the cup in my hand. Heaven. Perfect coffee. Absolute, bloody, heaven.

2.

A Heap of Stones

There are good things about growing up in a small village, you know everyone and they know you, the bad things are the same. Nobody ever forgets the time you let the chickens out, that Mrs Prentice had been raising, or that your dad was taken away in a police car, and never seen back in the village again.

I got a job, when I was old enough, just like everyone else did, at the factory which was the only employer in the area. I did the same work as everyone else for two years, and barely noticed the time passing, until one day, when I just couldn't do it anymore. I was tired of being the girl people still called Tommy Belton's daughter. He had been gone for years, but that was not enough. He could have been dead for all we knew.

The day I decided to stop going to work, I also decided to leave the village. I took every penny I had saved, and boarded a bus. I felt as though I was discovering new continents, brave and undaunted by having no plan, or definite destination. The town where the bus ended its journey seemed loud to my ears, used only to the rhythm of the place I had grown up. I had enough saved up to rent a room, and pay for a week up front. That would be sufficient time for me to find work, and maybe decide if I wanted to stay or go further.

I asked the man who rented the room to me if he knew anyone who was hiring, and he directed me to a noticeboard in a shop window. I had never been a waitress or a cook, but I took down the details, and considered if they would be better jobs than working in a factory. The woman in the café took me on as a waitress, and I learned the job. It was a little better than my previous job, and I got a meal as part of my pay, and kept my tips. Getting to know the customers was interesting too, and I found that chatting a little meant the tips were better.

A woman who came in every day, to eat her lunch, became a friend, and we talked a little, learning about each other, a snippet at a time. She worked in the lawyer's office across the street, and one day she told me that a client was looking for a caretaker to live in their home, and tend to their animals for six months while they were away. At the time I said nothing, but over the next few days I thought more and more about it, eventually asking if the place was still open.

I quit my job in the café, with a promise to come back if the place in the hills was no good. I knew it would be though. I was excited, and hopeful when my friend dropped me off there, and, although it was in an isolated spot, I loved it from the first moment I was there.

Each day after I had tended to the animals, and had my breakfast, I went for a walk, getting to know the area, until each tree and rock became more familiar to me than my face, or my hands.

It started with three stones. Balanced on a boulder, on a Tuesday. When I went for my usual walk, I noticed them and they made me smile. The next day there were two more. I was intrigued. Why were they doing it? I was excited to go out for a walk the next day. There were five more. Each day it grew and I began to add tiny stones as well. It became like a conversation, each of us adding a new piece of stone. Tiny pebbles and big rocks, all adding to the interaction. My curiosity about the other person involved was gnawing at me. I decided to find out, and waited in hiding until I saw him trudging up the hill. It had been nearly fifteen years, but I knew him.

He looked straight at me as he placed a pebble on the top of a wonky pile, waved his hand and disappeared. Tears coursed down my face. My Dad had brought me pebbles, and my heart had never been so grateful for anything.

Two days later I had a letter, left in the mailbox at the far end of the property. It might have been there a few days, I suppose, as I only checked it once a week. It came from the prison where my dad had been for fifteen years, and they regretted to inform me, that he had passed away.

They had no need to tell me. I already knew.

3.

A World Away

She had grown up free, and a little wild, out in the middle of nothing, people said. She saw the abundance, the huge variety of wildlife, and the joy of being able to run barefoot around the farm. The local school had been full of children like her, who rode before they could string a sentence together and knew how to deal with an occasional visiting snake on the property before they went to school. The heat was normal, and the flies were a constant that visitors noticed. Going to university was a shock to her system, she tried to fit in, and go to the parties, in the tight-fitting clothes and the shoes that pushed her toes into points, and lumps. She met the men who asked her to meet them, and was surprised when they wanted to kiss her, and sometimes more than that. It would only be a few years and she could go home, throw away the shoes and the dresses that squeezed her, and go back to being her.

When University was over, she heaved a small sigh of relief and drove herself home. Something had changed, and it was a surprise. Her Parents, it seemed, expected her to be a grown up, she should keep the shoes and the squeezed toes that went with them, and wear the dresses that restricted everything else.

A job at a school, which offered accommodation along with teaching experience came up, and she snatched it with both hands. She liked the girls she taught, and a few of the other teachers. Her timetable meant that she had time to paint, and a local sculptor offered her the use of his studio. Finding new ways to work with the clay, and learning to use the tools was a joy, and took up every moment that was not required by the school.

She met him through friends, and he was handsome, different from other men she had been out with. He asked her to marry him and there seemed no reason not to. Her family were less keen, but that was often the way with families. He had come half way around the world to meet her.

The situation in the country changed, politically. It was becoming an uncomfortable place to live if you were a liberal and believed in everyone having some freedom, and one day, pushing a pram through the crowds, she saw police officers behaving like thugs, bullies openly pushing and threatening. By the time he came home from work, she was in a terrible state, and they both knew it was time to do something. Their options were limited. They could stay, and try to fight what was happening. People were. Not people with families. Not people who had a baby in the house. Or they could leave.

That meant leaving her family, all of them. It was terrifying. The journey to where he had come from would take weeks, the boats set out full of people like them, who had seen what was coming and wanted no part of it. As always, she went to her father for advice. Arriving clutching her ticket, and dissolving into tears. They were due to sail in a week. He made her a cup of tea, his cure for everything, and sat her down, resting his grandson on his knee while she calmed herself.

"I will be so far away. I will miss you so much." She blew her nose and wiped her eyes.

"Darling girl. If you go into the kitchen, do I love you less? Or into town?" She shook her head. "Then go to his country, where you and this little boy will be safe. I will love you just the same, from here, from next door, or from the other side of the world. If you hate it, then you can come back, and you will have lost nothing." His hand was twice the size of hers, when he wrapped her hand in his. "I love you, darling girl, and I am proud of you. This is brave, but you are strong enough. I will come to the docks and wave until my arm falls off, and when I come to see you in your new home, you will meet me and wave the same way." He held her eyes until she nodded her agreement. "Every week I will write you long boring letters about what we are doing, and you will do the same. Nothing will change."

The voyage was rough, and they arrived in England in the cold and the rain. Her thin coat, stopped neither, and she owned no winter clothes. She wrapped everything she could find around the baby to keep him warm, and watched out of the window for the sun to shine through the grey clouds. The coal fire gave out very little heat, but she sat close to it and hoped that summer would come soon. Snow came first, and she cried, at the beauty of it, and the biting cold on her toes.

Every week she wrote a letter, on thin blue airmail paper which was cheaper to post, and, true to his word, every week her father did the same. Those letters became a lifeline to her, a brief trip home to the sunshine, and the people that she understood, without explanation.

Another baby arrived, after a short summer, and then the winter came again. She started to build a life, to meet friends, other women who were isolated, perhaps not so far from home, but still alone, and in need of support. They helped each other. When the children went to school, she began to teach a little, picking up her skills again. When Wednesday came, she sat down, and wrote her letter, all week, she saved little things to tell him, storing them away and pouring them onto the paper. His letter arrived each week, usually on a Friday, but not always.

Baby number three arrived in February, when the snow was thick on the ground, but the promise of spring lay ahead, and this time, it seemed that life was working a little better. Her parents would make the trip to visit. There would be more than a letter, there would be talking, and she would hold their hands, and they would be in her home. For weeks before they arrived, she walked on clouds, knowing where they were each day of their journey, and remembering her travels, made the countdown to their arrival easier to endure.

The docks were busy, but she had been there for an hour, and, although the children were bored, they were intrigued to meet their Grandparents, and watched the huge boat pulled in by ropes thicker than their arms. It took time for everyone to be allowed to get off, but when they did, and she was wrapped in their warmth, the wait and twenty times that long was worth it. They were delighted with their grandchildren, and stayed for weeks. It was a wonderful time in her life, when she could show them her new life, in the warm spring sunshine that felt like winter to them. The weeks ran out too fast, and before she was ready to let them go, she was standing on the docks, waving until her arm fell off.

Just as her third baby went to school, baby number four arrived. She was tied again, alone in the house with a squalling, sickly child. The world, meanwhile, moved on, and air travel was becoming more accessible. She dreamed of the day when she would be able to travel home in hours instead of weeks. Each Wednesday she sat and wrote, as she always had, and each weekend, she sat to read her father's letter to her. They had never wavered. Each letter ended the same way.

'No matter how far, Darling girl.'

They visited again, coming to an airport not the docks, but no less joyfully, they spent the summer, with the children on holidays from school, they sat in the garden, and enjoyed the time together, watching the babies become children before their eyes. The weather cooled as the children went back to school, and their grandparents went home to the warmer weather, leaving her alone again.

When her mother was ill, she left her children behind to fly and visit, but had to come back, to the responsibilities of children and work. Her mother died while she was on the other side of the world. The guilt she felt at not being there was sharp, taking her self-esteem and her coping skills to an all-time low.

The cost of telephone calls abroad dropped, and it seemed a minor miracle to be able to speak to her father, while he struggled with the loss of the woman he had loved for more than fifty years. Now, along with her letter every Wednesday, they took turns to call each other, on a Saturday morning, and those became the highlight of her week.

His letter arrived on a Tuesday, unusually early in the week. He wrote:

"Darling Girl, I have some things to tell you, remember when we talked about it making no difference whether you were in the next room or across the world? I know you do. I wanted to remind you, to make sure that you knew that it makes no difference if you are here, or gone to the next life. I love your mother as much as I ever have, and I feel her around me, enjoying the flowers in the garden, just as she did when she was here. Love doesn't change because we are not here. Don't forget it, my darling, wonderful girl. Kiss the children from me, and save one for you. Love, always. No matter how far, darling girl. Dad x"

It was his turn to phone on Saturday morning, but the call never came. When the clock ticked around to lunchtime, she dialled his number, but there was no answer. She tried again an hour later, but there was no reply, and there never would be again.

Alone, and never having felt so lonely, she looked for signs that he had told her the truth, that, wherever he was, he loved her still. That she was his darling girl. She found nothing.

A week passed, and she began to function a little better. A letter arrived from the lady who had cleaned his house, saying that, as requested she had cleaned out the property ready to be sold. She had shipped his personal things and they would arrive soon. The box that arrived was full of him, the smell of him, his old pipe, and a box of his favourite tobacco, a cardigan, worn thin with use, that she wrapped herself in, and felt a little safer. A bundle of her letters, that he had kept, his wrist watch, and an envelope, addressed in his familiar scrawl.

"Hello Darling girl. I have had a chat with Doris. You remember her, I think, the lady who has cleaned the house for me for years, anyway, I asked her to send you my things, once I am gone, and to put this letter in with them.

We have been so lucky, you and I, because we knew that we were loved. When you walked onto that boat, with your head held high, I was so proud of you. I wanted to shout and yell that you should stay, so that you would be close to me, but I knew your life was somewhere else. You'll know what I mean, when your children start to go off on their own.

If you are missing me, look at them. They all have a look of your Mum and me, and that, along with the love that I am sending still from wherever I end up, will be enough.

You'll always be my darling girl. Keep on being brave, and strong, and remember that you were, and always will be loved. No matter how far, darling girl. Dad x"

She sat and watched her children, and noticed the way they said some things the same way as her dad, how they had some of his ways of looking at life, how they stood up for people who were afraid. She nodded quietly to herself, and remembered all the years of letters, about what was happening in each other's lives. The things they would have talked about if she had stayed. They had still talked about them, but the chatting had happened on thin blue airmail paper, and later on the phone. Her children had better chances, because she had given up her homeland, her life had been harder in some ways and easier in others because of the choices she had made. The thing she was sure that she had not missed out on though, was the love and care of her Father, whether he was in the room with her, or half a world away, love is stronger than geography, and it turned out to be stronger than death too. Love is, when you come right down to it, all there is.

4.

Apple Cake

"Wow, that's good cake." He savoured the taste, the light texture, the balance between the fruit and the fluffy sponge. It was a wonderful sensation, buttery, and delicious. "Your cakes are always good, but this is a step beyond." Josh sat back from his empty plate, the table heaved with the remainders of the barbeque, wine glasses half way to empty and plates piled up. There had been ten of them for dinner, and the evening had been fun, everyone was smiling, as much from the company as from the wine, and the food. They knew each other well, and had for years. There had been meals just like this one in each one of their homes, but all of them agreed that the pudding was the best when Carrie was cooking. "What makes this cake so much better than anything else I've eaten?"

Carrie took a deep breath. "It's a very special cake. A very important cake Josh." The quiet conversations around the table stopped. Nine pairs of eyes turned towards her, something in the tone of her voice intrigued them. "OK I will tell you." She smiled at them, and sipped her wine.

"When I was young, my Mum, who was a wonderful woman in very many ways, but was completely rubbish at cooking, taught me a great many things, but I knew I would have to look elsewhere if I wanted to know about food. We lived in an area that was carved into fairly distinct communities, Irish on one side of us, and Jewish on the other. Being a skinny, annoying protestant English child gave me a foot in neither camp, but friends in both." She stood up to circle the table topping up glasses.

"My friend, Ellie, grew up in a loud, happy Jewish family, but, perhaps because the food they ate was always wonderful and flavourful she was completely uninterested in it. Her Mother and Grandmother cooked every day, and the smells and taste were beyond my comprehension and experience. Ellie's Grandma Reenie, was desperate to pass on a lifetime of cooking experience, but my friend's lack of interest was clear. One day when, once again Ellie had refused, I found the courage to meet the old lady's eyes, and ask if she would teach me. I think she was surprised, but she agreed, perhaps hoping it might spark some interest in Ellie. So, a week later I found my way to her house, and in the tiny kitchen I spent a very happy Sunday afternoon, learning how to make chicken soup, coming each week and making potato latkes and salt beef, baking challah, and flaky borekas. It was a joy, and while we cooked, we talked. She became my friend, and I think I became hers too." There was a wistful tone to her voice, and she paused to sip her wine and collect her thoughts. Around the table, her friends shifted in their seats, settling in to hear the rest of the story.

"After a while, I was getting better at the cooking, and learning the skills I had wanted so very badly. I arrived for my usual Sunday afternoon lesson, to find Reenie sitting at the table with a piece of paper in front of her. She pointed to the chair opposite her, and she smiled at me. She said that she was surprised that I had kept on coming for lessons, but the time had come to teach me the most important thing about cooking, and food and life." Carrie raised her eyebrows. "I waited for her to start, and was amazed to see her eyes were a little wet, as though she might be upset. I had never seen a grown-up cry, and I worried she was ill or something. I made her a cup of tea and put it in front of her, and she began. 'Today, we are going to cook apple cake. It's a very old recipe which was passed down through my family, Mother to Daughter, for as long as anyone has eaten cake. Today, I will pass the skills to you. Look after them, and one day, pass them to your children.' Her face was so serious, I was a little scared, but I nodded. 'This is my mother's handwriting.' She turned the paper to me, and it was faded, and not in English, there were hard lines through the paper and the writing where it had been folded. 'Long ago, when I was younger than you, my mother took me and my brother and sister to the train station, where a lady was waiting to take us to England. She hugged us, really hard, and told us to look after each other, that she would see us soon, and we would all be together. She had told us where she had sewn jewellery and precious things into our clothes, and reminded us to keep it all safe. Then she reminded me that the recipe for apple cake was sewn into the hem of my blouse. We were frightened and very young, but we climbed onto the train waving to her, and we came to England, with lots of other children. It was the last time I ever saw her.' Reenie's tears had fallen then, and I tried my best to comfort her. Eventually she sniffed and wiped her eyes, and carried on. 'This piece of paper is a symbol of hope and trust, she told me. My Mother knew that they had little chance to get out, they had paid a fortune to the government to buy our freedom, in the hope that we would be safe, and trusting that my Aunt Marion in England would care for us. At the bottom of the page, she wrote: There is no reason to share this wonderful cake with people who are unkind or intolerant or who bully or attack people for the sin of being born into a different religion or skin colour. Share this cake with people you love, bake in the love, it's stronger than hate. Taking this with you, darling Irena will make sure that Mr Hitler and his friends never taste the most wonderful cake in the world, which is revenge enough.'" Carrie watched their eyes around the table, and waited for what she had said to sink in.

"Food is about more than stopping people being hungry, you can do that with a sandwich. It's about a night like tonight, when friends get together to share food, to laugh, to enjoy each other's company. That was what I learned from Reenie, that was the real lesson, and that every single time she made apple cake, it was her own personal victory over the forces of darkness and destruction, that took her parents from her." Carrie sat back and sipped her wine.

"That's a hell of cake." Josh smiled. "So how did you learn how to make Italian food?" Carrie laughed out loud.

"Ah, there was an Italian family in our street, between the two communities, and the grandmother was wonderful." She twinkled back at him and topped up the glasses again. Somewhere out there, in the sparkling lights of the city, she thought she could hear Reenie's laughter and could feel her love. The fierce love that was the strongest of all weapons.

5.

Arts for Arts' Sake

The clouds were thick and heavy, hanging in purple swags across the top of the hills. Down in the valley I felt safe, as though the hills were gathering around me and keeping me safe. Whenever I have to go away, I come home to these hills, to my valley. To where I am safe and sound.

Except that the danger found its way into the valley, like a serpent winding its way around the edges of the hills. The danger came dressed in smiles and a good jacket, and threatened everything I had ever had or wanted.

The morning he arrived, the rain had been threatening and I had decided to work in the shed. I had cleared it the year before, and made it into a studio where I could work, and show my pieces, sometimes a tourist would drive through the valley, and see the sign advertising my studio, drive up the lane and take a look. That was the way the danger arrived, dressed like a tourist, and wrapped in friendly smiles.

He raved about my work, asked prices, seemed to truly enjoy the paintings, even the sculpture I thought was a complete mistake. I was really hopeful. Selling a couple of pieces would be wonderful. He promised a show, pieces in a gallery, fame, fortune. It turned out he was a bigger mistake than the sculpture.

His hair was brown, long, it hit the collar of his jacket, there was a wave to it. His eyes were very blue, and they shone down at me when he asked about the pieces, why I painted them. I tried to explain them, but it was hard to tell someone what I was feeling when I painted. If I was entirely honest, I had no idea how it worked.

That first day he bought a painting. I was so happy, I took the payment on his card, carefully checking his name, Ben Carlton. The bank would be pleased. Not excited, but at least less angry with me than they had been.

He came back a few weeks later and told me he had sold the picture, and made a profit. He wanted another one. That was fine with me, and I was happy when he chose one, and even happier when I saw the payment on my bank statement.

After that, he came once a week, and he bought something every time. I was painting, and selling it all, and the scary letters stopped arriving from the electric company. I was on a total high. I threw myself into the painting, spending days in the shed, coming back into the house only when I was too exhausted to carry on.

Once a week became twice a week. He was making a profit on every piece and the demand was rising. I was starting to feel pressured into producing more, faster, but I was already working as hard as I could. There was a part of me that was screaming to put the brakes on, to hold a part of myself back, safe. The other, much bigger part of me urged me on, remembering the pile of bills which used to sit on the door mat and shout at me.

As I painted, concentrating on not thinking about it, trying to relax and be free, those eyes of his would pop into my head, and challenge me to paint faster, to make something he could sell. The blue of his eyes challenging me to paint them, but nothing I tried worked. I could never capture the colour or the shape, or the glowing intensity of his eyes. The challenge drove me and I tried, I pushed myself, but nothing felt right, nothing worked. I felt as close to drowning as I ever had.

Each day I walked to the top of the hill and breathed in the clean fresh air before I started work. It cleared my head, but I had stopped seeing the clouds and the rain, I had even stopped noticing the smell of the grass after it rained, and I would never have believed that I could do that. One morning, I think it was a Thursday, I sat on the hill and watched his car drive along the lane. The damp from the grass I was sitting on seeped slowly through my paint splattered jeans. I could feel the clammy coldness on my skin, but I could not make myself care about it.

He climbed out of his car, and went straight to the shed, but I presume it did not take him long to work out that I was not there. He stood in the small yard, and turned to look at the hill. He knew where I would be. Perhaps he knew me better than I thought.

It took him a while to walk up the track. It was a steep climb and he was unfit. Too comfortable sitting in a gallery, never getting out to walk or push his feet up a hill, through damp grass.

His eyes glowed with annoyance, he had been forced to come to me.

"Where are the paintings?" He growled.

"I can't keep up this pace. I need a break." I sounded weak, even to my own ears.

"So, you are sitting on the wet grass to make yourself feel completely sad about life. What is the deal with artists?" He stormed at me. I felt the weight of his disapproval and anger.

"I am taking today off. I can't paint today." I met his eyes, those glowing, hard stones.

"Then paint me." He challenged. "Paint me. I'll sit for you."

It was what I had be waiting for, dreading, and pleading for in my heart, my soul. Yet now it was here, I felt as though I was standing on the edge of a cliff, the wind lifting my hair from my face. The fear holding me back and the need driving me on.

I stood up and walked down the hill. I could feel him following me. Feeling his anger coming at me in waves, but no longer afraid.

The easel, the blobs of colour, the brushes, my tools. He sat on a stool, one foot on the floor, and I painted, with every part of me, every bit of me poured into the paint, and onto the canvas. It was the best work I had ever done, and the worst day I had ever spent.

The canvas filled with colours and swirls and the eyes that glowed out at me, He sat and made no complaint. I painted and there were no words between us. The only sound was the rasp of my brush against the canvas. My breathing was shallow and quick as though I had been running.

When it was done, I walked away, exhausted, back to the house, I left him to it. I ran a bath and climbed in. When I was out, and dried, and wrapped in a thick dressing gown, I walked out into the shed, and he was gone, and so was the painting.

I sat on the stool where he had sat and wrapped the warmth of the soft fabric around me, and I was glad.

The next day, and the next, and the next found me in my garden, pulling out the weeds which I had left to grow untended. I mowed the grass and clipped the hedge, and the thorns cut my fingers, and the nettles stung my arms. I felt energised, stronger, and ready to go back to work. I pulled on my paint spattered jeans, and went to my shed, but nothing worked. I tried to paint a landscape, tried to catch the clouds that hung on the hills above me, but nothing worked. The next day, the same thing, and the next and the next.

After a week he phoned. He asked if I was painting. He laughed. It was a cruel hard sound.

I held the phone in my hand, and listened to him laughing. It went on for a long time, and I found that I was still listening to it, sitting on the floor in my living room with my back against the wall, and my hands over my ears. Even when I had hung up, and put the phone in the other room.

That night, I spent on the floor, in my living room, too tired, too empty to climb the stairs. My eyes were raw with tears, and I curled into myself and slept, pursued through my broken dreams by blazing blue eyes and sharp claws. I woke, exhausted, and aching, and was unable to keep even water in my belly, but by the time the sun went down, I felt a little better, cleaner, and slowly I was able to eat and drink a little.

Two days later, I tried to paint again. The colours spread across the canvas, and I made a half decent attempt at a landscape. It was nowhere near my usual standard, but it felt better. On the canvas, the sunlight broke through the clouds, and the green hills below were lit with the light that spilled through.

The light wrapped around me, and when the knocking came at the door, I ignored it, and painted. I painted as though my soul depended on it. Through the night and the darkest hours, I carried on, until there were five canvases leaning against the walls, and the first shafts of daylight crept through the windows, and the knocking on the door finally stopped.

I was back. I was myself again. The danger had come to the valley, to my home, and I had almost drowned in the fear, but I had come through it, and out the other side. That morning, when I walked up the hill to breathe the clean air and the fresh smell of damp grass, I walked with a clean soul, I would never be rich, or achieve any level of fame. My pictures would please some passers-by, perhaps even please them enough to pay my electricity bill, but never again would I be tempted by the dangerous possibilities which swept into my heart and my life with glowing blue eyes and tried to buy my paintings, and own my soul.

6.

Calling Time

The bar was full, customers made their way through the doors, enjoying the time spent together, and the drinks, the tills were ringing. The music from the juke box melted into the conversations and the gusts of laughter that blew through the room. Tom watched his clients enjoy the evening, and enjoyed it even more than they did. The kitchen sent out food orders and the bar staff filled glasses. Smiles thrown from one side of the bar to the other, waiters carrying trays and laughter to the tables.

His bar manager Lyn called him over to settle a complaint. The food was late, and the customer was unhappy. Tom smiled and smoothed the ruffled feathers. A discount was offered and accepted. Tom nodded to Lyn, and passed the receipt to her.

Leaving the hustle of the bar behind, he slipped into his office, and sat down, sipping from a coffee cup, and sorting through invoices, he kept an eye on the cctv on the monitor in his office. Which is why he saw the fight, not the very start, a punch or three had already been thrown when the movement caught his attention.

Out of the office and back into the bar, mentally shrugging, it happened. It was the industry he worked in. The two guys were throwing unconvincing punches. Most fights were over quickly. Tom pulled and pushed his way through.

"Enough." He caught eye contact with both of the fighters. "Time to go." Both guys argued their reasons to stay, but Tom had rules, and the first one was that fighting was bad for business. He nodded to James, who had worked behind the bar nearly a year and they escorted the two men to the front door, Tom shooting a foul glare at the door staff who should have been dealing with the problem.

The guys were still grumbling, but they headed in different directions, and Tom gave the nod to the two burly guys on the door. Neither one of the fighters was to be allowed back in. He would be having a chat about why he had to dive in to stop a fight when he paid wages for door staff.

Pushing through the double doors, he found the bar back in full swing. Nothing out of the normal way of things. His phone buzzed in his pocket and he slipped it out, and opened the message. He was late with his loan payment. He knew that. He hoped, that after he had paid the wages tonight there would be enough to cover the loan.

The evening rumbled towards closing, and everyone laughed, and drank their last drink, and finally went home. The staff cleaned up, and he paid their wages, cash, not one of them would be paying tax on their earnings. He counted what was left, it was nearly enough, he was short a couple of hundred. He made the call he was dreading as he locked the door behind James. He had given up his flat, and moved into the back room to save money, until the loan was paid off. He had been there over a year now, and although he mostly made his payments on time, he still owed more than he had borrowed.

"Do you have the money?" No greeting, no small talk.

"I do. I've been working hard the last few days. Can I bring it to you in the morning?" Tom was tired and what he wanted most to do was to crawl into his bed and sleep not drag himself across town to see the man he hated most in the world.

"I tell you what, Tommy boy. I will call round to see you in the morning. You can pay me then, and I'll have a cup of coffee with you too. There's something we need to discuss." The voice sounded as though it had been soaked in whisky and filtered through gravel. Tom agreed, although his choices were limited.

In the morning, with a cup of coffee inside him, and an envelope holding his loan payment, he considered himself ready to meet the man who let himself in through the back door, which was left open for him to make a discrete arrival.

"Tommy?" He reminded Tom of a shark with small teeth, bared in the semblance of a smile.

"Craig, good to see you." It was a lie, both of them knew it.

"I need to ask you a favour. I need you to drop a package off for me. I'm getting too much attention, and everyone knows my guys, you're nobody, you're not known." He watched Tom's eyes, and saw the hesitation. "I'll ignore the fact that your payment was late this month, to sweeten the deal, and I'll make next month's payment myself." The shark's teeth smile was back.

"I've never got involved in anything like that." Tom poured coffee, and passed the cup across the bar.

"Never delivered a parcel for a friend." Craig shook his head as though he was disappointed.

"Do I have a choice?" Tom's shoulders slumped.

"No. Not at all." Craig's eyes were hard, like bullets.

"Where does it have to go?" Resignation dropped his shoulders.

"Good boy Tommy." Craig slurped from his cup. "Great coffee." He pulled a scrap of paper out of his pocket and pushed it across the table, and a small package from his other pocket. "Before the end of the day, please." He tapped his hands on the bar, grabbed the envelope, and walked through to the back door.

Tom opened a cupboard behind the bar and found a pair of thin vinyl gloves, slipping his hands inside. He was not going to leave any evidence that he had touched anything. Taking a breath, a deep sad gust of air dragged into his lungs, he collected the address and the parcel one in each gloved hand, and slid both into a plastic bin liner, checking the address. He knew the area, and the road, he would have to look for the house.

The journey was uneventful, and he pulled up in a comfortable looking neighbourhood, where the house he was to deliver to sat back from the road, he left his car on the street and, still wearing the gloves, he carried the parcel. He rang the bell and waited. A woman answered the door, and he smiled.

"Hi. Courier. Parcel from Craig." She nodded, smiled and took the parcel. He stepped away from the door and walked away. That was it. Tom thanked everything in the universe.

He climbed into his car, stripped the gloves off, and dropped them into the bin liner. The piece of paper with the address on it was still in there, and he balled the whole thing up and pushed it under the seat. He would look for a rubbish bin to get rid of it.

He turned left, and right, as a precaution to make sure there was nobody following him. He was fine.

At the junction with the main road, his heart stopped. A line of police cars and two vans waited, ready to pounce. He sat still in the junction, waiting for someone to flash blue lights, or wail a siren, but nothing happened. His heart beat fast, and his breath was shallow, cold sweat trickled between his shoulder blades, but nothing happened. He watched a uniformed officer walk down the pavement, and signal to the others. They moved off as one, and turned the corner, into the street he had just left. It could be a coincidence, of course it could. The chances were, however, against it. He indicated away from the line of police cars and pulled out onto the main road. His breathing slowed, his heart came back to a reasonable rate, and he drove at exactly one mile below the speed limit all the way home.

In the bar, grabbing a newspaper he pushed out into the beer garden, where he crumpled the paper, throwing it into the barbecue pit they used through the summer. He lit the paper, setting it blazing, before he added the bag with the gloves and address, standing to watch them burn, until only a pile of ashes was left. He mixed and crushed the ashes and swept them carefully into a dustpan, before sprinkling them carefully into the big commercial bin at the back of the bar.

His phone was ringing when he came back inside. He was not surprised to see Craig's name on the screen.

"All done?" He asked. No chit chat.

"Yeah." Tom was not going to admit seeing the police.

"Thanks mate." He hung up.

The night flew past, and the takings were good. Tom sat alone at the end of the evening, the bar was clean and the takings were in the bag ready to go to the bank, sitting on the floor in his bedroom. A quiet knock on the front door took him by surprise. He checked the cctv. Craig was standing on the doorstep, cringing away from being asked to do another favour and knowing that he could not pretend to be out, Tom's steps were slow.

He opened the door, and stepped back, watching Craig land on the floor.

"Shit, Craig." He put his hand on the man's shoulder, thinking he had drunk too much, but the greyness of his skin told him a different story. Tom grabbed the collar of Craig's coat, and pulled the man in so that he could lock the door. He opened the front of Craig's coat, and found the wound. It was an easy search. The dark red stain on the white shirt told of a large amount of blood already lost. "Craig, can you hear me? I've got to call the ambulance. I can't fix this one." The eyes that looked back at him were unfocused, and glassy.

Tom grabbed his phone and called for an ambulance. They arrived less than two minutes later, but the time seemed long to Tom. His mind raced with questions. He was no friend of Craig's, the man would not come here by choice. Craig was a career criminal, he had, presumably a great many enemies, who would be glad to see him gone, but why would he land up on the doorstep of Tom's bar?

The ambulance crew took Craig away, with blue lights and sirens. The police arrived and took photos of the floor, the walls, the cloths Tom had used to try to stop the bleeding. They talked to Tom, and told him they would be back, and followed the ambulance in the hope of being able to talk to Craig.

Tom cleaned up, the floor, the cloths, the door, his shirt, and finally himself in the shower. He made himself a coffee and sat at a table. A movement by the front door reminded him that he had left the cctv monitor on. A heavy-set man stood on the step, and Tom watched with curiosity as he pushed his weight against the lock. At the same time, a noise from behind him told him that someone was kicking in the back door. He was angry, no he was furious. His day had been a new low, and he had tried hard to deal with it, and keep himself safe. Whoever was planning on coming into his bar, had better expect a headache.

Tom hefted the baseball bat which lived behind the bar, in case of just this sort of incident. He stood to the side of the double front doors, and watched the lock give a little each time it was pushed. From the back of the building, he heard another kick, but he knew that was a strong metal door, and it would take a little while.

When the lock gave, he was ready, and he met the intruder with a good hard swing of the bat, sending him sprawling across the floor. Tom kicked the man's shoulder, turning him onto his back, and sending his butcher's knife skittering towards Tom. Losing the tenuous grip he had on his temper, he hit down hard on the hand that had held the knife. The man groaned, and Tom smiled. There was no longer any kicking going on at the back of the building, which either meant the other person was inside, or had given up and run around to the front. Tom stepped away from the door and waited. It was not a long wait, a shorter, slimmer man slipped through the door, almost falling over the heavy-set guy on the floor. Tom connected the bat with his shoulder as he was stumbling. He cursed loudly and fell heavily to the floor, with another blow to the head making sure he stayed there.

For a few minutes, Tom thought hard about what his next step should be. Craig was a bad guy, that was for sure, but he was a bad guy Tom knew, if something happened to Craig, there would be new, unknown, maybe worse guys taking his place. On the other hand, the two on the floor, neither of whom he recognised, who would be waking up shortly with headaches, were here for a reason, not to rob him, that was sure, not with Craig stabbed on his doorstep. There had to be a connection.

Tom decided to take the offensive. He poked the smaller of the two men with his bat.

"Hey?" He asked. The man replied with a groan. Tom raised the bat, ready to hit again, and the man pulled an arm across his face. "OK, so we know you are awake. Why are you here?"

"Looking for Craig. He came down here, to see you. He was raging, but he never came back." The man spat blood from his mouth.

"He's in the hospital, somebody stabbed him, he landed on my doorstep, bleeding his guts out. If what you are saying is true, you will pick up Godzilla over there, and get out of my bar." In the end Tom had to help him drag the big one out onto the pavement, before slamming his door, and fetching some wood from the shed to screw up the broken doors until he could get a proper job done in the morning. He checked the back door, which was still holding, and cleaned his floor again, before washing his hands, and making a fresh cup of coffee. This was not over, and he was going to be ready for whatever came next.

The sky began to lose the dark edges, and still Tom sat. Eventually the phone rang. He slid his finger slowly across the screen.

"Tommy?"

"Yes."

"Thanks. I was all for blaming you, my clients had a visit just after you. I thought you dropped me in it. The client caught up with me, before I got to you. They arrested him. They told me he slipped out of a raid earlier today, his wife got taken in. They were laughing, saying they'd been watching the house for months, they'd only pulled surveillance off this morning so that the raid wouldn't be compromised. You were a lucky boy." There was a pause while he took some slow breaths. "You saved me Tommy. I owe you. No more debt. It's gone, mate."

"No more favours?" Tom pushed his advantage.

"No more. Jimmy and Mick just turned up. You smacked them up." He laughed a little.

"Bye Craig." Tom heard the phone disconnect.

Exhausted, Tom slid between the sheets, hoping for a few hours of rest, if not sleep, but he slept long and deep. Safe in the knowledge that the danger was over.

She looked like her sister. Same height, similar build, her hair was a little longer, and her fuse a good deal shorter. They had grown up on hard streets, where you stood your ground or expected a beating. Revenge was a norm, and punishment for grassing up family was swift and brutal.

The petrol that glugged through the letterbox in the early morning before people were on their way to work, landed and spread across the flooring, the petrol-soaked rag sparked and the roar and cackle told her that honour had been satisfied.

Tom heard the roar, he dreamed he was being chased by a lion, the roar shaking the ground and the power of the animal making his heart beat hard against his chest. He sat up, sweating, and smelled the smoke. Hearing the sounds of explosion and breaking glass he knew the fire had reached the bar area, and his only chance was to leave through the back door, if he could reach it before the fire got there.

He slipped into the corridor, not sure if someone would be waiting for him on the other side of the door, but without any choice. He grabbed the cash bag, and threw open the back door. The alley was empty. He stepped out into the bright sunshine, hearing sirens screaming towards him again, this time on top of fire engines. It would never be over. He shrugged his shoulders, and turning away from the high street left the bar and the problems behind him. He could deal with it later. He could rebuild. He might even sell the plot and move away, maybe a new city, maybe even a different business. The night had changed things. He was free to make different choices.

7.

Dear God

The cold air made his breath puff out in clouds. His scarf caught in the wind, and wrapped around his face, his hands deep in his pockets. The tops of his ears were cold, he could feel them tingling with every step he took. The key was wrapped tightly in his hand. He was looking forward to a cup of tea, and maybe a biscuit. His hands felt the soft roundness of his paunch, and he reconsidered.

The door opened easily, and he stepped into the warm, still air. The mail was on the mat, three envelopes. He carried them through to the office via the kitchen. His desk was covered but he found a gap, and put down the hot cup. The first two were clearly bills so he put them on the pile and moved onto the other. The one in a plain envelope, a hand written address on the front. It said 'To God.' He took a sip of his tea, and wondered what he was supposed to do with it. It wasn't addressed to him, but he was the vicar, and so he worked for, perhaps even, represented God in the neighbourhood. He propped the envelope up on his desk and chewed his lip. He needed to take advice on this one. He had no right to interfere between a parishioner, and the big fella. On the other hand, someone out there, had reached out, maybe looking for help, or reassurance, and that was definitely his job.

He ran his hand through his hair, leaving it sticking up. Unlocking the inter-communicating door to the church, the hush of the sacred space reached out to him. His footsteps whispered across the wide old flag stones. The smell of wood polish from years of loving cleaning filled his senses. He knelt at the altar, his head bowed, chatting, in his headspace, to an old friend, a loving father. He placed the envelope on the rail, between his elbows.

"What should I do with this?" He asked. His eyes flickered. He considered the possibilities, hoping for some inspiration. Slowly he turned it over, and run his finger under the flap. Still time to change his mind.

Inside was a letter, written in a wide looping style, over two pages. He stood, took two steps back from the altar, and bowed his head. Tucking the letter into his jacket pocket, he went to find some biscuits.

At his desk, he pushed the creases out of the pages, and sipped his fresh cup of tea. He started to read.

Dear God,

I know we haven't spoken for a while, I'm sorry, that's down to me. Funny how I've spoken to you, when things are really scary, like when I thought the kids were really ill, or when I needed, really needed, to find the money for the gas bill. I've kept you for emergencies.

I suppose this feels like it's urgent, and I don't know how to fix it. I need some help. I hope, really hope that you're there.

I know I'm lucky. I know I have two great kids. I have had years of great times with them, and they are wonderful people, but they are both at university now. I see them in the holidays, they have their own lives, and they should, but I don't. I go to work, I pay the bills, I sit. I'm embarrassed, shamed, by my loneliness. I look at people, with their friends laughing, and I resent them, I'm paralysed by my solitude.

I watched my marriage fall apart. I saw how it dented my children. I did that to them. I accept responsibility for it. It was my decision, to be with him, to have kids with him, to give them him as a father, I knew that he was irresponsible, but I thought

I could be sensible enough for both of us, then for all of us. I thought that I could build a family and keep them safe.

They're wonderful, I'm so proud of them, and I'm trying to step back, let them be free, without their over-protective Mum standing over them. That leaves me standing on my own in the shadows. It's dark, and I can't find a way out, or a way on from here. Can you help me, to turn the light on?

I wondered about maybe meeting someone, a man, I mean, someone who might care about me, for me, not because they're hungry, or they need collecting from somewhere. Just for me. Someone who might want to wrap themselves around me, to keep me warm and safe. Cliché, I know. 'Empty nester seeks love.' Hardly headline news. It feels disloyal, like I'm replacing them. Am I? Do I just need someone, doesn't matter who?

I need help, and I've read all the self-help stuff and tried to learn how to meditate, which, by the way, was not a success. Joined the gym, which was good, but to be honest, being lonely on a treadmill, or a bike, is the same as being lonely at home, and tiring too.

I looked after my Mum, when she was ill, and now she's gone too. I used to run all the time, from one job to the next, fitting in everyone, and tired all the time, but now I sit, and have all the time I wanted so badly then, but I have nothing to do with it, and nobody to share it with.

I think this has helped, writing down how I have been feeling, so whatever happens next, that has to be a positive thing.

I don't expect a miracle, like someone will knock on my door and want to be in my life, just, can you show me a sign, that you're there, that I'm not completely alone in the universe tonight, because that's how I feel.

I really hope you're there.

N xx

◆ ◆ ◆

He read it through twice, wiping his eyes, and sniffing. It was a cry for help, and he would gladly give it, but there was no clue how to find this woman. His thoughts ran over the things she had said, perhaps she had been brought up believing, but had lost her faith along the way. It sounded as though she had been battered through life. He wanted so much to find her. He was going to have to think about this some more. Give her a sign, she had said. How on earth could he do that? He folded her letter and tucked it into his jacket pocket to read it again later, and to keep it private.

His 'to do' list was long that morning, he hadn't started writing his sermon, and there were letters to reply to, apart from the one which had touched him this morning. He had two hospital visits to make, and a few hours to spend at the hospice. He checked his watch, and gathered himself, he needed to get out of the building before the toddler group arrived.

His phone rang just as he was reversing out of his parking space, so he drove back in and turned off the engine before answering.

"Hello."

"James? Hello, It's Simon, have you got a minute?" The bishop's assistant always started conversations like this, as though James had a choice.

"Yes, of course. How can I help?" James caught sight of his hair in the rear-view mirror and smoothed it down.

"I'm phoning around to ask if any of our churches would like some signs."

"Signs?"

"Yes, you know the sort of thing, encouraging people to pop into the church, friendly, jolly sort of things for outside. We have banners, which might work best for you, with your railings.

What do you think?" He was waiting, James could hear him tapping the phone.

"Yes please, I would very much like all the signs you can let me have." It's a sign. James shook his head. Could it be that simple? She had asked for a sign.

"Oh, really? Well good, I'll drop them over for you this afternoon to the vicarage. Thank you."

"No, thank you." James bit his fingernail, a habit he was trying to break, and smiled to himself in the mirror. "A sign." He told himself.

The hospital and the hospice visits were done, and he was on his way home, excited to see what had been left for him.

The vicarage, was in fact, a very small terraced house which was always a bit on the chilly side in the winter. He kept his jumper on, and pulled the banners and signs out, laying them on the floor so he could have a look.

'Come on in and wish me a Happy Birthday'. The first one read, obviously for Christmas. 'Sunday services everyone welcome', 'Step inside for peace and cake', 'Love is the only thing that is important', 'God is Love', 'Friendship and Fellowship evening every Tuesday everyone welcome', 'Bring me your burdens and I will carry them for you'. They were all good, but not what he needed. There were two left, one big banner and one small one, he unrolled the big banner, and there it was. James rocked back on his heels, amazed and delighted, and a little emotional. 'Thanks for the letters, come on in for a chat.' Reaching for the small one he spread it out and laughed loud and from the heart. 'Jumble sale this Saturday.' Perfect.

It couldn't wait until the morning, he carried the banners down to the church and tied it to the railings, it was perfect. He was delighted with it. He picked up another, and tied that on too, then another, so that the railings were almost invisible behind the messages. He was smiling, widely, and he was a little warmer inside his jumper and his coat, than was comfortable, but he felt good. He hoped that she would see them, and understand.

◆ ◆ ◆

What had she been thinking? What had possessed her to write all those embarrassing things about herself and then deliver them through a door, where a perfect stranger could read them. It was toe curling in the extreme. She had even walked past two other churches, deciding that they didn't look like God would live there. She was losing the plot, that was for sure.

The dog was trying to dance about, wanting to look excited, but it was hard with his legs stiff with old age. She knelt to rub his hips and shoulders, before she pulled her coat on, and clipped on his lead. He trotted after her, though the dark streets, stopping for him to sniff, and pee.

The wind had picked up and her head was down, burrowed deep into the hood of her coat. A swirl of leaves lifted by a gust twisted through the air past her. Nearly home, she slowed her pace, the dog was older and slower now. Coming level with the church, and the site of her ridiculous behaviour, she felt almost angry with herself. She looked down at the little wiry haired animal who was her best friend, and smiled.

The dog stopped, turned around and barked, he had seen movement, even though his eyes were not as sharp as they had been in his younger days, a flapping sign still caught his attention. She turned with him.

There it was. Thank you for the letters, come on in for a chat. She stood absolutely still, she had asked for a sign, and here it was. It was crazy. She laughed, loud in the silence. Tomorrow, she had a day off from work, she would pop in to the church then. Hugging the plan to herself, she set off again, through the cold back to her house, which was warm and waiting for her.

Not feeling so stupid now.

In the morning, she stepped out, with purpose in her stride, she had missed that, for how long? Too long. The church door was open, for a moment, maybe a bit longer, she stared at the coir matting, where her letter must have landed. The smell reminded her of younger days, with her Mum, holding hands and sitting quietly. The inner doors were panelled with glass, and she pushed one open and went through, finding a polished wooden seat, smoothed by hundreds of bottoms over centuries of prayer and hope, and buffed by caring dusters. Her eyes scanned up to the vaulted ceiling, and the detailing picked out in gold, against the soft cream of the plasterwork. A man walked in, from a side door, walking almost silently on the worn stones of the floor. He knelt at the altar, his head bowed, his hands resting open on the rail, his body still. He wore a jumper that had seen better days, or maybe had been washed too much. His hair was spiky, as though he had forgotten to brush it that morning. She watched his peaceful prayers, and wished she felt that certain. She breathed slowly feeling her heart slow and her body lose some of its tension. A single tear slipped over the edge of her eyelid, finding a path across her cheek, towards her jawline.

He stood up, bowing, to the altar, and turned towards her. His smile was wide, and welcoming. He looked, she considered the word she would use to describe him. Wholesome?

"Hello." He covered the ground between them with quick easy strides. "Would you like to talk, or did you come in looking for some peace?"

"Um, the sign said, come in for a chat?" Had she misunderstood?

"Would you like a cup of tea? Chatting's always better with tea." His voice was gentle, but not cloying. She felt safe.

"Thank you, that's kind."

"Come on through, then, I'll put the kettle on. I'm James by the way, James Renton, I'm the vicar here." He walked back through the side door, and led her into a kitchen, where he busied himself with tea.

"Naomi." She said. "I'm Naomi." She leant against the door frame, watching him putting out cups and saucers, shaking her head at the offer of sugar, nodding at the milk.

"So, you liked my sign? I'm glad, the bishop only sent them through to me yesterday. Have a seat." They sat at the table, a wipe clean lump of plastic-coated wood.

"Yes, I do like your sign. It's very welcoming. I haven't been in a church for a long time. I used to go with my Mum when I was a kid, but then life gets busy and it's all a bit hectic." She shrugged.

"I know. So does the big fella." He nodded towards the ceiling. "He doesn't get offended that we don't talk to him every day, but every now and then, he likes to hear from us, just to let him know, if we're OK, or if we need any help, you know, normal stuff."

"Is that what you tell him? Normal stuff?" She was curious now.

"Yes, I tell him my worries, and my fears. I tell him about the people I visited in hospital yesterday who are scared and feeling ill, and maybe in need of a bit of support. This morning I told him I had forgotten to buy peanut butter too, because I was angry with myself about it. Just chatting really." He sipped his tea.

"You're absolutely sure he's there?" She shrugged her coat off onto the back of her chair.

"Oh yes. It's me I'm not sure about." He raised his eyebrows and smiled. She noticed that there were dimples in his cheeks, and that he had missed a tiny patch when he shaved this morning. She laughed, and it surprised her. "Tell me about yourself, Naomi."

"Nothing to tell, my kids, a boy and a girl, are grown up, moved out, I have a job, in town, and a small slightly smelly dog called doughnut." She smiled too. "I'm really glad I came in today."

"Me too. Will you come back, another visit, do you think?" She nodded. "Good. We're here for services on Sundays, and there are things going on all week, evenings, afternoons, and if you want a chat, I'm here most mornings."

"Thank you. I'll pop back in." She pushed her chair back.

"Um. If you're free, probably not, but if you were free, and felt like it, I was planning to go to the cinema tonight, and I'd much prefer to go with you, than on my own." He held her gaze with his.

"I, er, well."

"No, it's fine. I just thought." He studied his hands very intensely.

"I'd love to. What time." She smiled across the table, surprising herself by accepting.

"Really? Wonderful, OK, It starts at seven thirty so shall I pick you up at seven?" He beamed at her. "You asked me what I talked to him about earlier? I asked him to find a lovely girl that might like to go to the cinema with me. Don't you tell me that he's not real!" His clear pale blue eyes sparkled at her, and she found that she was smiling too.

8.

Flowers from the Market

The bottle was halfway to empty. I had hoped that I would feel less by now, but the pain continued, the numbing I had anticipated stayed out of reach, and the pain seared my heart.

The day had been long, and there was more to come. It started so well. I had eaten a healthy breakfast, avoiding the pitfalls which tempted me. I had smiled at the right times and given the correct response as often as I could. My life, in short, had been on track. I had almost been paying attention. Not enough, as it turned out. Breakfast, had been the highlight of the day.

As it was Saturday, I had time to do some browsing, walking slowly through the market, laughing and choosing food for dinner, and buying the enormous metal key which for some strange reason had called to me. The market was set up on the high street, canopies over the stalls, and hustle and bustle. Jimmy went to the flower stall, while I was looking at the keys, and bought me a bunch of mixed blooms. I should look up the names of the flowers. They lay on my kitchen table, a little crushed, but smelling wonderful. The stall holder who was selling me the key made an "Ahh" face, when Jimmy passed me the flowers, and leaned in for a kiss. He smelled of his aftershave, breakfast, and something that was uniquely him. I smiled into his mouth. He was, I told myself, a good man. His deep brown eyes burned into mine, promising more than flowers. I had loved him for fifteen years, and every year seemed better than the last. We were like swans, perfect on the surface, running so hard beneath the water in the darkness.

They poured out of the building society onto the pavement, directly where we were standing. The man cannoned into Jimmy knocking him and me onto the ground. I was shocked, stunned. Jimmy, not so much. He was back on his feet almost before I was aware we had landed. Chest out, head high. He was a lion, an alpha male, a man. He just happened to run into a man who was angry, full of adrenaline and carrying a shotgun. He took the blast straight in the chest. I watched his body crumple. Knees first, landing hard. Then down, lying next to me, his eyes open. I crawled to him, wanting to protect him, make him better. The bag that fell from the robber's hands landed between me and Jimmy, and I covered it with my body, as I pulled myself to him. He was gone. His eyes, which had laughed down into mine so many times were empty. His mouth, which I had kissed so many times was still. There was blood. So much blood, and screaming. It took a while before I realized it was me.

There were all sorts of things that had to happen. The police, the ambulance, I had to go to the hospital with Jimmy even though it was clear there was nothing they could do. Eventually I was able to go home. The pain, the long, harsh unbelievable amount of pain surrounded me. I waited. I knew that he would come. I welcomed his coming. After all, I had something of his. I had stolen from them, and they had stolen from me.

I heard a noise. Nothing strange, just someone moving around near the back door. We lived far away from anyone else. More accurately, I lived far away from anyone else.

The pistol my father had brought home from the Falklands, that we had hidden for all the years since he had died, had suddenly become my best friend. The bottle of brandy was on the kitchen table. My glass was empty. The pistol, not so much. I knew how to load it. I knew where the bullets were kept. Bring it, the fuck, on.

"Do you want the money?" I shouted. I was loud. I knew that, but I was angry. The voice that came back was one that was entirely new to me.

"All I want is the money, I don't want to hurt you."

"Too fucking late." I no longer cared.

I heard them? Him? No idea. Moving through from the conservatory towards the kitchen. I stood up. I had no business being this angry, but that is very rarely something that stops rage.

"The money is in here, with me." I stepped away from the table, and into the corner of the room, with the walls on both sides of me. "If you want it. Come and get it."

I could hear whoever it was moving through the house towards the kitchen. The lights were low. Not a problem for me. I knew the house. I knew the kitchen. I could care less if I lived or died.

I watched the barrel of his gun come into the room first. I was still. I was more still than I had ever been. The barrel was followed by the rest of the gun, then his hands. His arms. I watched them sweep the room.

"I'm here, as arranged."

"The money's on the table. From the bank, and the extra three. That's what we agreed." My hand wrapped around the gun in my pocket and made me feel safer.

"That's great. Only one thing. The price has gone up. There needs to be another three." He held his hands out to his sides, as though it was something out of his control.

"We had a deal." I breathed, carefully.

"Things change." He shrugged. "We want to keep this between us. The extra three will keep my mouth shut."

"What guarantee do I have that you won't come back for more?"

"You're not buying a washing-machine, it doesn't come with a guarantee." He smiled. I saw the light glint on his teeth, and I knew he would come back, time and again.

"OK. Fair enough. Grab the money and I'll take you to get the other three." He followed me out of the door, into the darkness and the sweet smell of the garden.

"You keep your money in the garden?" His voice lifted with incredulity.

"You wouldn't have thought of it, and you're a thief." I heard him shrug, his jacket shifting fabric against fabric. I knew the garden, he had never been there before, which was why he didn't see the hole in my veggie patch until he was right on top of it.

"What the fuck?" He turned to me, and I squeezed the trigger. I was surprised at how loud it was, and that I had done it at all. Easy to plan it before he arrived. Easy to dig the hole. Easy to tell myself that it was my back up plan, in case he tried to turn the tables on me. The bloom of the blood on his shirt was dark against the white tee shirt he wore under the open jacket. He watched me. Shock written on every feature of his face. I watched him too.

Jimmy had been unfaithful. He had told me, apologised, told me it was over. He had promised. I had believed him, and I forgave him. Really meant it. The trouble is that forgiveness, means that you move past the offence, not that you go blind or deaf. I went into town to get my hair done that afternoon. Jimmy was supposed to be meeting a client. I saw them sitting outside a pub, and watched quietly while my insides shrivelled, and I hoped, against all sense that I was mistaken. Following them to a hotel, cheap, not very clean, and with a bored receptionist who let me past, so that I could hear what they were doing. It was loud, and heart-breaking.

Dragging the body was hard, but I talked to Jimmy the whole time. Tipping him in, I told myself that it was fair. Jimmy had speared my heart. He had killed Jimmy. I had killed him. He would grow my vegetables. I filled the hole, and replanted the vegetables on top. Fuck it. Revenge was supposed to make it better. It tasted like I had been throwing up all night.

The last of the brandy was waiting for me. After I had cleaned the kitchen floor. After I had hosed the path, and the grass. The sun came up and found me drinking the last of the brandy. I raised my glass to Jimmy, and to the life we could have had. It would be a life on my own, from now on, but there would be no lies. I would be me, no compromises.

I hung the key I bought in the market that morning above the front door in my house. A friend asked me what it unlocked. I told them, and it was the truth, I suppose, that it was the key to my heart, and it belonged to me.

9.

Freddie's Fish Finger

Yesterday It was all going so well. My life was happily dull. I have never understood why people complain about routine.

I had volunteered, as I did every time it had to be done, to clean the deep fat fryer where I worked. Nobody else liked the job, but to me, there was a joyful rhythm in the emptying, cleaning, scrubbing, and finally refilling, alone in the shop, with the radio playing quietly. It took time, but it was wonderfully satisfying.

I started early in the day, because it had to be completed before the fryers were needed for lunchtime. I wore my work overall, the really thick one. It would be a dirty job, and I always ended up getting splashed with the oil. The first job was to drain the huge vat. The hose slipped and slopped easily into the first empty can. The others were lined up and ready. The smell of used oil, dirty in the air made me wrinkle my nose.

Once the can was full, I stopped the flow and hefted the heavy can out of the way. The flow began again until the fryer was empty. The filter was next. It sat at the bottom of the fryer in a few inches of oil, and caught the bits of chicken, fish and stray chips that were missed, and bits of batter and breadcrumbs. I pulled out the filter, and slid it into the tray, where it would drip while I cleaned everything else. I was nearing the half way point, so I made myself a cup of tea. The radio was playing a gentle love song which I half remembered from when love songs mattered to me.

My back ached a little, the big cans were heavy. I rested back against the counter, and smiled at my distorted reflection in the stainless steel, while I sipped. I loved the shop when it was quiet like this, no customers shouting their orders, nobody pushing and shoving to get the orders out. People walked past the big window, bent into their umbrellas against the weather. It was dreadful yesterday.

I fetched the degreaser and pulled on my rubber gloves and washed and scrubbed, rinsed, scrubbed, rinsed again, until the walls and the base of the fryer were clean.

The roll of kitchen paper was on the side, and I grabbed it and wiped the surfaces dry, leaning deep and wide across the fryer. The stainless steel shone in the overhead lights. The covers which sat over the top of the fryer sunk below the soapy water, and I moved on to the filter. It should have dripped through by now.

The drip tray was full of oil, dark and thick with the food that had bubbled in it, which needed to be tipped carefully into the last empty tin.

I was nearly there. My tea, when I tasted it was cold. I made a face. I would make a fresh one when the job was finished.

The filter was the last job. It was full. I was surprised, every time I did this job, how much fell off and floated away, over cooked dark brown pieces of batter, and nearly black chips. The food that slowly rots in the oil if left, and turns it rancid and sour.

The filter needed to be emptied into the food waste, and it would be too heavy to do it in one go. Using the chip scoop, I shovelled the smelly mess into the food waste bin. If I could have done it in one lift, I suppose I would not have spotted it. But I did. It was lying on the top of a glistening mound of dark brown scraps.

I backed away, feeling sick. We had sold food from that fryer. How long had it been in there, floating around with the chips? Perhaps, more importantly, where had it come from? My phone was where I had left it, and I picked it up, dialling my boss. His phone went to voicemail, and I sat back against the counter.

"Freddie! Call me back, it's important. I'm in the shop. Please hurry up." I tried again and again, but there was no answer.

I wanted to run, to be out in the rain with the rest of the world, but I was fascinated. There were plastic bags on the side, so I pulled one off the roll and picked it up with the bag.

It was a finger, a human finger. There was no way we could open for lunch now.

My boss lived upstairs from the shop, he still had not answered the phone, so I would have to go and bang on the door and wake him. I tucked the finger under a dishcloth, it felt wrong to leave it exposed. I slipped out through the back door into the alley, and stood under the cover of the porch, banging on the door to the flat. Nothing. He must be dead to the world.

Then I saw the blood splashes on the door frame. If there had been no porch, the rain would have washed it away. There was a tremor in my hand when I pulled it back from the door. I needed help. Three steps took me back inside. I expected to be alone, but I had company.

The man standing in front of the counter was almost as wide as he was tall, and he was very tall.

"Sorry we aren't open." My eyes ran over the dishcloth under which there was a fried finger. "Cleaning the fryers today." His eyes were very still and he watched me with an intensity I found very difficult.

"Freddie worked for me. He's gone." His voice was low, but clear.

"Gone?" I heard the wobble in my voice. If I did, then certainly he would have.

"Very conscientious, coming in early to clean the fryers. I like that in a potential manager." I stood very still. Did he just suggest I might be the manager? Where had Freddie gone? Or did he mean gone as in dead?

"I have always liked to clean the fryers. I know that's a bit odd."

I shrugged. I watched his eyes, there was no life in them, just concentration.

"I can see how it would be satisfying. Do you want the job, Janice?" He almost smiled. All mouth, no eyes.

"Do I get a pay rise?" He nodded.

"Yes. Quite a good one. You just need to have the money you have taken through the till ready every Friday, and the till rolls. I do the books, everything else. OK?" I nodded. He smiled. "There is one other thing. Freddie left something behind. Did you find it?" The intense stare was back. Did he want me to tell him I found the finger? I lifted the dishcloth, revealing the tip of the finger, and checked his expression. He nodded. "Yes, that's what I'm looking for, and you've put it in a bag, how convenient." He held his hand out, and waited until I dropped the bag into his hand. "Good luck in your new job Janice. Nice work on the fryers." He slipped the finger into his pocket. Making me admit that I had found it, and not told anyone else. Making me complicit. Making me the Manager.

The clean oil glugged into the fryer, and I checked the time. I had an hour. The oil would be hot enough for lunch.

10.

Golden Leaves

The leaves were golden brown and orange, pushed by the wind into piles, and lying thick on the woodland floor. They walked through the quiet afternoon, the chill seeping into their hands and feet, and making their cheeks glow. The two little boys ran through the woods, pretending to shoot each other from behind trees, laughing and throwing leaves at each other, filling the quiet afternoon with their happy noise and bustle.

The sun was low in the sky when they walked back through the gathering dusk to the house, where there was hot chocolate to drink, and dinner to eat, and then blankets and cuddles on the sofa in front of a favourite movie.

They did it every weekend. It was their thing. Sunday afternoon at three. Sometimes, when their Daddy was at home, they all went. In the summer they ran in shorts and t-shirts. In the spring they walked past the fields where lambs played, and in winter they ran through the frosts and sometimes the snow. In autumn, though, when the leaves were thick, and the air was cold, it was the best of times.

Later when they were older, they walked, sometimes talking, sometimes in silence, but they still walked together. They spent the time together, and often it was the best time to thrash out things that might have grown into an argument at home, here in the woods they found the space to talk things out. Even later, they went away, to study, and came home in the holidays to walk and tell her about the new friends, the new life, and the things that they were learning. She noticed there were more gaps. Pieces of their lives they kept to themselves, and that was the way of the world, but she felt the space which grew between them.

While they were gone, she walked with their dad. Together they rekindled that part of their life which had been going on in the background, the spaces which the children had filled, and then emptied when they left to live their own lives, in which their parents were less and less involved.

The days she spent, walking through the woods were happy, and she remembered her children chasing each other through the trees. She shared hot chocolate with her husband, and long-distance phone calls with her sons.

When her sons brought home girlfriends, she smiled, and welcomed with open arms, some she liked, some less so. It made no difference, they would choose who to spend their lives with, and that was exactly as it should be. Whether she liked them or not was irrelevant. Each year that passed brought a different girl, for each of them, until they found people that they truly loved.

There were weddings. She bought the right dress, for each one, and watched her beautiful sons become someone else's life. She held tight to her husband and smiled in the photographs that they would hang in silver frames, to remind them of the day, and of the family that she had helped to grow.

When grandchildren started to arrive, she took them with her when they visited, through the woods, lifting them onto the fence to wave at the lambs, and pushing through the leaves and home for hot chocolate and warm blankets on colder visits. When they were far away, she walked with her husband, until he got less strong, and one day he stayed asleep, no matter how hard she tried to wake him.

Slowly, she fought her way back from the sadness that engulfed her. She walked alone through the woods that she had loved all her life. She walked through the cold bare trees, trimmed with the thick white frost. She saw the trees push out their leaves in the spring, and the lush green in the summer, when the leaves began to turn colour and drift down from the branches, she walked, remembering the days when they were a family, and when three o'clock on a Sunday afternoon meant wrapping up in coats and scarves and heading out to the woods.

It was five to three on Sunday, and she already had her coat on, when their cars pulled onto the drive. Both families spilling out. She was pleased to see them, of course she was, and she pulled her coat off and wrapped the grandchildren in hugs and was surrounded by her family. Her two daughters-in-law, unloaded the cars, and went to the kitchen, shooing her, and her sons, and her grandsons out. They helped her into her coat, and walked to the woods. Her sons walked with her, while the children ran ahead, pretending to shoot each other from behind the trees. Screaming their joy and freedom. It was cold and crisp, and her cheeks were soon pink, and her hands and feet felt the chill. They talked about everything, and nothing, and she was back to where she had always wanted to be. The space that had been, had diminished and they were back with her, laughing and teasing each other, and telling her about their lives and what was happening with them again.

Heading back down the hill towards a dinner cooked and waiting, and mugs of hot chocolate was the perfect end, to a perfect day, a life filled with memories, and with a future to make more.

11.

Memory

I woke up, and the house was sunny, it was late, and I had slept on, my eyes newly open from sleep, squinted in the brightness. My feet, slipping out of the covers and onto the carpet, toes warm and soft, walking through the squares of light and shadow on the carpet, sunshine at the window. Across to the door, and out into the hallway, without touching anything, slipping through the space. Half way down the stairs, I could tell the house was empty. Not entirely, I could hear my Mum singing. She had a low strong voice, not a song I recognized. Her singing felt so personal, so private, I sat down, not wanting to intrude, or to burst the bubble of her happy place. The door to the kitchen was open, her notes seemed to drift out on the sunshine, swirling around me, making me feel excluded, and jealous of her happiness at being alone, but at the same time, not wanting to take it from her, recognizing it as rare, and a treat for her. Was that when it began? Did I see her then, as someone in need of protection? Perhaps. I was a smartass kid.

If I saw my mother as needing protection, what did I see as the danger? My Father was difficult, a complicated man, perhaps that is with the benefit of hindsight. As a child I saw him as the angry one, the shouter. Cruel. The one who created an atmosphere, made everyone in the family on edge, pushed us to compete, to attack each other. Looking back, I can see that he was angry, maybe scared, a lot of the time. I expect that four kids, and it's hard for me to say, but a wife who he loved, but was childlike, and sometimes irresponsible, but always beautiful and funny. His life maybe came with more stress than I understood at the time. The truth is, it's hard to see your parents as a real people, because they aren't, they are the parts of themselves that they choose to show to you, and you have no control over that, because you are a child, and they are grown-ups. They have all the power, and you have none, except that once you are a grown-up yourself, and you are a parent, you see your children for what they are, hugely powerful, god-like in their demands, and your reaction to them. The only protection parents have from the tiny despots who live in their houses, is to keep their power a secret from them. It is a smoke and mirrors transaction, one that you know will be discovered, and yet we all do the same. Loving a child, to the point of being fully prepared, on a daily basis, to lay down your life to prevent them ever having the sniffles, and trying to show them the right way to be a human, are almost entirely opposed ideas.

Bare toes crossing the warm wooden floor from the bottom of the stairs to the kitchen door. A creak of the boards alerted her to my presence. Her face was wide and smiling, as she snatched me up into her arms, kissing my cheek and wrapping me in a hug that feels warm and safe. She ruffled my hair and called me sleepy-head. She put me down onto the bench next to the table, the thin fabric of my nightie wrapped around my legs, while she made toast, dripping with butter, and marmalade. The window was high up, and all I could see through it was sky, and a few fluffy clouds. Each bit of toast was thick with butter and sweet marmalade. The crusts of the toast were burned in places. My Mum's toast, there was no toast better in the world. Licking crumbs and melted butter from my fingers.

I was allowed to choose my own clothes that day, and after checking that I was not being watched, I wore the same underwear as the day before, and pulled shorts and a t-shirt over the top. My hair had not seen a brush in a while, and I had worn no shoes for days, my father would have said I was running wild, I saw it differently. My sisters and brother would wrinkle their noses and call me a stinky animal. I was allowed to play barefoot in the garden, running over the sun-warmed concrete, and the springy grass, climbing the garden gate to sit on the pavement and eat a frozen lolly. Riding my bike, stabilizers tipping me left and right, and stopping underneath the kitchen window, to hear the happy notes drift out onto the summer morning, knowing that she was happy again, and that I had helped her to stay that way.

Later, perhaps forty years after that morning, when I sat in the nursing home with her, and she had no language anymore, knew no words, she still smiled the same way when I spoke her name, and somewhere in her mind, scrambled though it was, I believe that she remembered the little child, and I remembered the woman in the prime of her life who sang songs in her sunny kitchen. The bonds made on that day, and thousands of others just like it, kept me sitting in an uncomfortable chair, taking care of her, always feeling responsible, as though her problems were my fault.

Years later, when she had gone, I still remembered that vibrant beautiful woman, who grabbed the freedom of an hour without her kids and her husband, to be herself, and I hoped I did enough.

Now that I am the old lady, and I look back on more than I have ahead of me, now that my children watch me carefully for signs that I am not coping, for signs I may be less able or less strong, and I wonder if they remember snatched days when I was young and strong, and they were tiny despots who did not know their strength. I close my eyes, my eyelids paper thin against the sunshine. In the quiet of the afternoon, I strain for the sound of a low strong voice, singing a song I still do not recognize. I can almost hear it, hanging on the sunshine just out of my hearing, just a note here and there.

I wonder if she loved me, in the same way as I love my children, did it tear at her, and keep her awake at night worrying, did she wrap her arms around me and feel her heart beat on my breath, and did the warmth of my laugher keep her from the cold places in her soul? I hope it did, I hope I gave her that.

12.

My Brothers' Keeper

He always was surprised by the quiet. Outside cars and lorries thundered past, and the busy pavement was filled with shoppers. In here, in his wonderful old church, where he felt the love and protection of God all around him, was quiet and peace. He wished, he prayed and he tried his best, that his congregation was larger, that they were younger, and that they came to church to find more than protection. This was, however, a neighbourhood where safety was high on everyone's wish list. The streets after dark were dangerous, and gang activity was high. Only this morning, he had visited a local primary school to talk to the children about the gangs, and how to avoid being talked into them. He felt he was fighting a losing battle. The gangs offered respect, money, power. Only once they were in, did the children realize the cost.

He knelt at the altar, searching his heart and asking for help. He felt helpless in the face of the power of the local gangs, and yet, compelled to try. He has officiated at too many funerals since he had arrived here, for children who had seen too little of life, and tried to console their parents when no words or prayers could support their grief.

He heard the front door open and close, the noise of the traffic seeping in and then sealed off, and stayed where he was. Finishing his time with God, with a prayer of thanks, he made the sign of the cross and stood, bowing his head for a moment.

"You been talking bad about me?" The voice filled the space. He turned to find a young man, probably barely out of his teens standing in the aisle, feet planted wide, chest thrust out. He was in ready to fight mode.

"How could I? I have no idea who you are." The priest tilted his head sideways. "I'm Peter Bradshaw. I am the priest here. Who are you?"

"No business of yours, old man." He shrugged his shoulders in a studied attitude of dismissal. "You bad mouth the gang, you bad mouth me. I am the gang, the gang is me."

"Ah. I see the problem. Yes, I have been talking to primary school children to warn them about the gangs. I have no way of knowing how successful I have been. It's my job." The priest sat down in the front pew and held his hand out to welcome the young man to take a seat with him.

"You need to stop talking to the kids, or I will stop you." The anger in his eyes, sparked across the space.

"The trouble is, I owe more respect to my boss than to you. My job is to protect the kids from the life you want for them. I want better for them." He threw a smile across the gap at the young man. "Come and sit down. Let's talk about it."

"No talking. Just stop doing it." The young man threw himself across the church.

"I'm flattered that you think I am making such a difference. Enough to warrant a visit from you. Thank you for that. I was just considering whether what I was doing stood any chance at all." The priest smiled.

"You're married. What you're doing is putting her in danger." A nasty lift of his lip accompanied the threat.

"If I phoned my wife now, and told her what you said, I can tell you what she would say." He raised an eyebrow. "She would invite you for dinner. She would tell me you needed something to eat, and for people to love you." He nodded to himself. "She would be right."

"You understand what will happen, if you carry on?" The young man stood, in battle ready mode again.

"Give me a chance to change your mind?" The priest suggested. "You came here today looking for power. Let me introduce you to the biggest power, the highest power. The strength that comes from love, not fear. The reason I can tell you that I will carry on, and you will not stop me by threats, to me, or to my wife, because I am protected by more than a knife or a gun. If you want real power, you came to the right place." The priest crossed the gap between them. "I know you have a weapon on you, but you cannot hurt my soul. Only the body my soul lives in." He was within a few feet of the young man. "Give it your best shot." He held his hands out to his sides.

"What?" The young man's bravado and swagger competed with shock. This was clearly a new experience. People cowered, or came at him armed. This man stood with no protection except his belief. If he could convince his gang members to that sort of conviction, he could run the city.

"Right, so, shall we have a coffee, or a tea, I think there is some fizzy drink here somewhere?" The priest walked away from the confrontation, and into a small room off the church, where there was a kettle. He made two cups of tea and put on in front of each of them. "I am guessing that you are high up in the gang. I understand that you are recruiting young kids to run drugs and guns around for you. I'm going to ask you not to, and also, I would like you and I to be friends. You do me this favour, as a friend, and I will be your friend. When you next get arrested, I will stand up in court and speak on your behalf, because we are friends." The face across the table from him softened a little, and he picked up the tea.

"My Mum used to drink tea like this." A smile took years from his features, then disappeared. The scowl descended again.

"Do you see her often?" The priest pushed biscuits across the table and watched two disappear.

"Not much since she died, four years ago." He cracked a well-practiced smile, which he believed would hide the pain.

"I am so sorry for your loss. That must have been difficult for you. May I ask how she died?" The priest leaned his hand across the table.

"Gun shot wounds. That'll do it." He smirked. "Pops was a little peeved at finding her with another guy. He took them both out, and then turned the gun on himself. I was asleep in the next room with my brother. My brother's still with social services. I got out. I made my own way. All I'm offering those kids you are so worried about, is a way to make their own choices, to make their own money and work their way up, the same way I did." He sipped the tea.

"What if I could find your brother? Put you back in touch with him?" The priest watched the cocky expression change.

"I would like to see him. He could come to live with me. I can afford it. I have two kids of my own. I pay for them." His chest puffed out. Pride? A demand for respect?

"What happens next for you?" The priest's voice was quiet. "The gang is for the young, how long do you have left of being useful? What happens when you hit your twenties? Will you see your thirties?"

"I'm strong. I'm protected." Another biscuit disappeared.

"But others would like to stand in your shoes?" The priest tilted his head.

"I won't die in my bed, an old man, but I'm strong for now. I'll get out before I put myself in danger. My kids, my woman, we can go away, leave it all behind, once I get enough money together. If you find my brother, I could take him away too." He stood, pacing. "Yes, good. Find him. Tell me where he is. I'll come back next week. Have an address for me."

"I'll see if I can find out where he is. They might allow you to visit. I don't know." What name would I ask for?

"Mark Gillan. I'm Danny." He nodded to the priest.

"Good to meet you, Danny." The priest held out his hand, and waited. The young man hesitated to put his hand out. Slowly he lifted his into the priest's, and shook.

They walked together to the front door, and the priest watched bravado and swagger carry the young man down the street. The traffic thundered past and maybe that was what distracted him. The teenager in a hoodie who loped across the road, dodging cars and vans, brought a blade and determination with him, and having delivered his message, ran away down the street, leaving Danny Gillan bleeding onto the concrete.

The priest ran, as fast as he could, dialling for an ambulance as he ran.

"Danny. I've called for an ambulance. They're on the way. Hold on." He pressed his hands down onto the wound to stem the blood flow. Their eyes met.

"You were right, priest. Find Markie for me, give him the life you talked about. You and me are friends, right?" The pain and fear in his eyes stripped away the swagger.

"I'm your friend, stay with me Danny." The priest held tight.

"He cut me up inside, I won't make it." He winced with pain. "I've seen enough of these. Just promise me, you'll find Markie, before they do. Let him follow you, not me." His hand reached out, and gripped the priest around the wrist.

"I will. I promise. Listen Danny, the sirens, they're nearly here." The grip around his wrist slackened, and the young man who had been so strong, was gone.

The priest sat back on his heels, and laid the dead boy's hands across his chest, he covered them with his own, the smears of blood mingling between them. He prayed with all his heart and soul, begging for understanding for the child who had been pushed into being a man before he was ready, and who had made bad choices.

The paramedics took him, and Peter walked back into the church. He washed the blood from his hands, and changed his clothes. He knelt at the altar and repeated his prayers, wiping the tears that fell for the waste of a life, and the lack of chances the boy had been given. He bowed his head and finished his prayers, then dialled the number he had for social services. He was a man of his word, and he would find Mark Gillan if it was at all possible.

The social worker checked the records, and quickly found him. He was on the foster list. An appointment was made and the wheels were set in motion. He stood and made his way towards the door to the street. Turning to the altar, to make his last bow, he saw the sunlight stream in through the stained glass, throwing coloured light across the aisle. He smiled to himself.

A promise made, and kept. A prayer answered.

13.

One for the Road

It was nearly closing time, at the Pirate's Head, and the regulars peeled themselves from their bar stools, out into the night where the rain fell gently. Shouting their goodbyes, and their hoots of laughter. Stella shrugged her shoulders. Another night, another load into the glasswasher. The till was full enough, and if her life was a little empty, that was her choice. The night had been the same as most, some arguments, a few songs. She had steadily poured their drinks, smiled, and taken their money.

The towels smelled of stale beer, and the drip trays waited for their turn in the washer. She had performed the shutting down routine too many times to have to think about it. The door was locked against the weather and anyone who might want to relieve her of the night's takings. The cash was counted and locked into the safe. She was almost done. Just the bar and the tables to wash, and the floor behind the bar to mop, and her bed beckoned.

The cloth, smelling of fresh cleaning fluid slipped easily across the bar in her hand, and the steam rose from the bucket. She mopped the tiles on the floor, concentrating on the beer spills which were sticky underfoot. The smell hit her all the harder, because she had been smelling the sweet floral bubbles in her bucket. Nose wrinkling decay and rot assaulted her.

The man sat in the shadows at the end of the bar. One arm resting on the surface she had just cleaned, and a glass in front of him.

"We're closed. You'll have to go." She told him. He lifted his head to meet her stare, and his mouth lifted into a smile.

"This is my place." His voice cracked, dry and underused. He tipped the drink and pushed the glass towards her. It was straight sided, not like any she had in the pub.

"No, mate, this is my place. My name is over the door. Time you went home." He was not the first punter she had stood her ground with over the years.

"My name is over the door too." He laughed. "I am the Pirate. They named this place for me, because they were so shitty scared of me. They took my money, when I had it, and bought my plunder when I had no gold. They sold me their women and their ale, until I had no more to give, then they sold me to the militia. I dangled just down the street. My feet danced to a merry tune, and I had to learn to be without breath in my lungs."

"You're telling me you're a ghost." She laughed. "OK, nice try." She huffed a smile. "Just for sheer cheek, I'll share a drink with you. What will you have?"

"Rum. In my glass." She picked up his glass, and washed it in the sink, drying it with a cloth, and keeping her eyes firmly fixed on him, she poured him a good measure of dark rum. She poured another for herself, and carried the glasses to his end of the bar.

He sipped, and smiled. "Thank you, woman."

"Stella." She corrected him. "Tell me where you sailed to then, if you are a pirate."

"I sailed around the world and back again, I miss the sea, the smell of the salt in the air and the feel of the swell under my feet. I miss the women, in Jamaica and Tortuga, but I am stuck here, where I fell in love, and swore I would not leave." She topped up his glass, and he raised it in salute. "Her name was Lucy, and she worked here in this place. She took my heart, as sure as the militia took my breath. They took her too. The night they came here to take me in. They took us both to the castle out by the river, and locked us up. She begged for my life. I heard her. They wanted me to hear, what she begged, and what they did to her that night. I swore, on that dark damp floor that I would hunt them down, each one of them, and I would kill them for what they did to her." He sipped.

"Not much you could do if they hung you, I suppose." Stella topped up his drink. She loved a good story, and she would make him leave when he had finished it.

"I haunted them, hunted them. Every one of them met a sorry end. My Lucy was never the same. She died not too long later. She cried as she lay dying, for me to watch over the little ones. She had given life to three children of mine. One girl died of a fever when she was just a babe, the other two grew strong, here, in this place, where Lucy's Father was the brewer. My son left and went to sea. He left no children, but a girl every port. My daughter, though, she had children, and grandchildren. She lived near here. I have watched over every one of them, all through their lives. Helped them through to the other side, when the time came."

"So, what brings you here tonight?" She poured the last of the bottle into his glass.

"You are my daughter's descendant. I knew it had come full circle when you took over this place. You have no children, last of the line. My work is done. Tonight, we cross together, and I can see my Lucy again. You were right, it is time to go home, I am tired and I am ready." Stella stood back from the bar, horrified, pushing herself away from him, shaking her head.

"No, I'm not ready to go." He smiled gently, and pointed to the floor. Behind her, she saw her body, curled up next to the mop bucket. "I wasn't ill. What if I say no? Refuse to go?" Her chin jutted out in rebellion. He recognized the look.

"You're already gone. If you won't go. We both stay, and we do nothing, just sit and watch the world carry on without us. I've waited a few hundred years. I'll wait more if you want me to." She stayed silent, but her eyes filled with tears. "I wrapped myself around you to keep the pain away, as I did for your mother. It may have slowed it down, and given you a little longer. T'is time."

He held out his hand and she swallowed, taking a last look at her body and her bar. Her hand in his, they walked through the front door, and into the life beyond.

14.

The Prodigal Son

"Rachel!" He looked across three rows of tomatoes at me, looking no different from when he was eight years old, and I had caught him with his hand in Mum's purse.

"What are you doing here?" My voice was low and I was keeping my temper in check, for the moment.

"That's a nice welcome." He smiled the lopsided smile which I am sure worked wonders on women who were not his sister. "I wanted to see you."

"People who want to see me usually knock on the front door, not skulk about in my greenhouses at a quarter to one in the morning." I raised an eyebrow at him.

"Not your greenhouses, this is still the family business." He turned to face me.

"Not since I bought Dad out. These are all mine. You should watch your step, I bought Dad's guns too." I met his glare with one of my own. We had always been good glarers, as a family. "So, if you're here to collect on your inheritance, there isn't one. The farm was on the brink of bankruptcy, when I bought Dad out, and I've turned it back into something worth having, on my own, so you can go back to wherever you've been the last twelve years."

"I'm sorry I wasn't here when Mum and Dad died. I should have been." He at least had the grace to look as though he was genuinely sorry. I believed none of it, but I nodded anyway.

"Back to my question. What are you doing in my greenhouse in the middle of the night?" I looked around me. "Have you stolen my crop?" I watched his eyes. This was more than just a few bags of tomatoes. His eyes slid sideways. "Looking for possible escape routes?" He froze. "I've worked really hard to build this up. I had to borrow to build each one of these greenhouses. I start early every morning, and finish late every night, but I'm turning a corner. I'm paying the loan and just about keeping everything going. I can't afford you messing it up. Please Liam."

"Look. Rachel, I know we were never close, but I found this thing, that makes loads of money, but I don't know how to do this stuff, and you clearly do." He put his hands out to his sides, taking in the whole greenhouse full of strong robust plants.

"You never listened when Dad talked to us about how plants grow." I huffed, remembering my brother skulking off while I listened to Dad explain about how it all worked.

"You did though. You're good at this." He tipped his head sideways. "Please help me, Rachel. I'll split the profit with you, half each." He chewed his lower lip. "It could help you, with the loans and everything."

I thought about it. The loan payments were huge. I needed money. I was so tired of working so very hard. I was running uphill, with my feet glued to the floor, and I was doing the best I could, but it was so difficult.

"Show me. I'm not promising." I followed him to the back end of the greenhouse, where he had moved my tomatoes sideways, and in their place stood twenty of the scrawniest plants I had ever seen. I ran my hand over one of them. "What have you done to them? They look sick." The soil in the pot was dry to my touch, and the leaves were rolled in on themselves.

"I put the seeds in the soil, like the book said. I watered them and I thought that would be enough." He shrugged.

"They're drugs, aren't they?" I smelled my hands. The heavy oily smell hung on my skin.

"They're cannabis." He whispered.

"I should call the police." I told him.

"I'll only disappear if you do, and they are, after all, on your land." He smiled. "Who knows how many other plants there are for them to find?"

"You really are a shit." I told him. "How long is it supposed to take, to harvest?"

"Once they are mature, the book says every six weeks." He held out a well-thumbed paperback.

"I'll get them to the first harvest for you, then you and they disappear. Once you pay me half." I held my hand out to him, it was the only deal I was offering. "Or they die, and they will, quite soon." He took my hand and shook it.

Luckily for me, out of my five greenhouses, the one my brother had been in had no tomatoes ready to be picked, so it was easy to keep the two girls who picked for me out of the way. I filled the trough at the end of the greenhouse and plunged the pots containing the scrawny plants into the water until bubbles came out, so that I knew the water had found it's way into every gap. I added them into the irrigation line along with the tomatoes, and turned on the mist as I left the greenhouse. I left it on for a few hours and then turned it off, and, as the sun went down, I carried on picking the tomatoes in another greenhouse, and loading the boxes ready for the morning. My crop went to the markets, and were mostly bought by restaurants. Supermarkets were interested in cheap fruit and vegetables, available all year round, not too worried about the taste. Mine were sweet, and picked perfectly ripe. They were in the market before the bloom was off them. They were also expensive. I also grew blueberries and raspberries, and some strawberries.

Before I went to bed, I checked in on his plants. They already looked a little more cheerful. The leaves had unfurled, and spread into their well-known palmate shape. He was standing on the doorstep when I got back to the house.

"They're looking better. I'll phone you when the buds arrive." I nodded and opened the door.

"Can I come in? Cuppa?" He looked rumpled.

"Cuppa." I confirmed.

"Thanks Rachel." He followed me into the kitchen, and watched me make tea. I put the cup in front of him, and slipped bread into the toaster. When the machine popped, I buttered the toast, and pushed it across the table to him. I'm no chef. It was as close to a dinner as I would get most days. He ate. Me too. "Can I stay?" I closed my eyes. I had been waiting for this.

"You can stay tonight. Your old room. There are blankets in the cupboard." I watched him think about it. "I am doing this to help both of us, but that doesn't make me happy about it."

The days ticked past in the same way they usually did. Early starts, picking, packing. Cutting out extra shoots, to encourage the tomatoes to grow. Late finishes. My brother was gone for a few weeks, then turned up late one night. His plants were getting big and fat. The leaves were thick and plentiful, and the start of buds were pushing out. He whistled low, in the gathering darkness.

"Rachel. You have a way with you. They look just like the ones in the book." He gently stroked the leaves through his fingers. It made me catch my breath, he looked so like Dad. He stayed for the night, in his old room, and he was gone when I came back to the house for lunch.

The day that they were ready, the buds, fat and oily, I picked them and lay them out on tissue paper, in a greenhouse where the strawberries had already been picked, and the air was dry. I pruned back the leaves, and laid them out as well. I called him and told him he had a few days to wait.

On the Saturday he arrived and bagged what I had dried. He left to meet the buyer. I waited, sitting in the kitchen, and I think a part of me knew that he would not be coming back. I smiled when the hands on the clock hit midnight. My brother was a short-term sort of guy. He had never been ready to do the work, day in, day out. I knew that, and so had my parents.

I pulled my phone out, and dialled the number I had taken from his phone on the last night he had stayed over.

"Hello." There was a grunt the other end. "Liam dropped you off something today?" An affirmative sort of grunt. "I'm the grower. If you want more, I'll have some available in six weeks, or thereabouts."

"Liam gave you my number?" He asked.

"Yes. Is that a problem?" I asked.

"No. Phone me when you're ready." He took a puff of whatever it was he was smoking. "And every six weeks after that?"

"You have a deal." I told him. Long term. That's always been my way.

15.

Purple Shoes

The clouds hid the moon, and the rain fell, without mercy, or care. Her umbrella was, however, big enough, and her coat was wrapped tightly around her. After she left the car in the lane outside the gates, she settled the umbrella against her shoulder, holding it with one hand. Folding her fingers around the handle of an overnight bag, she walked up the driveway, which was long, but that suited her purposes. There were bushes on either side, and she was glad of the heavy Wellington boots she wore, making her way through the wet grass.

She pushed her bag up to her elbow and pulled her phone out of her coat pocket, tapping in the number.

"I'm here."

"Great, let me know when you're done." He took a deep drag on whatever he was smoking, she heard the sharp intake of breath.

"That's not how it works, you know that." Came her sing song voice. "If you want to book a service, you have to pay the bill." There was a pause, it was awkward, but not for her.

"Okay. It's done."

A message came through on her phone. Payment received.

She hung up, slipping the phone into her bag. The building ahead was well lit, and grand, if a little faded, it was the perfect place for a weekend away.

The front entrance was busy, someone on the front desk, a restaurant filled with people, a bar, not right up her alley. She turned left from the drive before she reached the parking area and walked around the building. The door to the kitchen was open, someone was being shouted at. She kept walking to the fire escape, and pulled the door open.

With a smile, she closed her umbrella and slipped inside. Two floors up on the back stairs, she slipped open her overnight bag, sliding her feet out of the rubber boots, and into the purple high heels that had been sent to her specially for this job, from her bag. The boots slid into the bag, and she checked her lipstick in the hallway mirror, pouting a kiss at her reflection, she pushed her heavy dark curls out of her face, slipped her bag and the umbrella into the housekeeping cupboard, took a breath, and knocked on the door.

"Yeah?" The man inside sounded like he was seriously pissed off.

"Hi. Jimmy asked me to come and see you." Listening to him moving to the door, she imagined he was looking through the peephole, and smiled straight at him, if that was where he was. The lock clicked and the door swung open, halfway.

"Jimmy told you I would be here?" The forty-something man was heavy set, with hands like shovels, he watched her from beneath his furrowed brows.

"He sent me as a gift, to you." Standing in the corridor, with his bedroom door open but his hand against the lock, she slowly untied the belt to her coat, and let the sides fall open, never taking her eyes off his face.

His eyes widened, his mouth gaped open.

She was wearing nothing underneath.

"Purple shoes." He whispered, to himself.

"You know what they say, the customer gets what he likes." She smiled, resting her hand on her hip. "Do you want me to stand in the hallway, or shall I come in?"

"Sorry, of course, please come in." He walked back into the room, and she kicked the door shut behind her.

"Would you like a drink?" Lifting a bottle of brandy, he waved it a little from side to side. She nodded. He poured two generous drinks, and put one on the bedside table for her.

"You have me at something of a disadvantage, I think." She traced a finger slowly from the tip of her chin down to her belly button. Her body was taught from hours in the gym, she knew he was watching. She slipped the coat off her shoulders, his eyes followed every movement. The rounded muscle across her shoulders, and her arms, the tight breasts, the flat stomach, where her finger stayed. She held her hand out, it was his turn. He pulled at his shirt, buttons flying left and right, he was fighting with the buckle on his belt, when she slipped her coat a little lower, making him stop and stand still, turning her back to him, with the coat scooping the base of her spine, and lifting one foot slightly out of the shoe. The shoes had come with instructions, to slip one foot out, slowly, so that he could see her heel and the arch of her instep. He drew in a gasp of breath, as she continued her turn, her hand dipping into the pocket, bringing out a small calibre weapon, complete with silencer.

He was still looking hopeful of a good time when he hit the bed. Small calibre, no exit wound. No mess, no clean up, less noise than popping a champagne cork.

Careful to touch nothing in the room, using her coat sleeve to open the door, she was gone, leaving him staring at the ceiling with dead eyes. In the housekeeping room she changed quickly into jeans and a sweatshirt, with a waterproof jacket over the top. Slipping her feet back into the rubber boots, loading the coat and shoes into the bag, and leaving the way she had arrived, walking slowly.

Back at the car, she hit redial. "It's done." She waited to hear that he understood, then dropped the phone and hit it hard with the heel of her purple shoe, smashing the screen. Pushing the shoe back into the bag, she drove past a charity shop, and left them the coat and shoes as a gift.

Pulling up on the driveway, no make-up on, her hair in a ponytail, and climbing out of the car, she heard the front door open, and two kids threw themselves out at her.

"Hello my lovelies." They wrapped their arms around her, laughing together.

"Thanks for having them, Mum. Sorry, I have to get going." The kids were already climbing into the back of the car.

"Good weekend love?"

"Yeah, thanks, nice to catch up with the girls, get dressed up, and wear heels for a change." She laughed, and her Mum laughed with her, but they were laughing at different jokes.

16.

Small Treasures

The box sat in the very middle of my dressing table, where it had been for years, since the day I moved in to my own place, and before that, at my Mum's house. A pretty little box, with a lid that opened and closed on a hinge, where my favourite things were kept. None of them were very valuable to anyone else, but they were to me.

I pulled open the lid and slipped them out onto my hand. A tiny fake flower that had been in my hair when I was a bridesmaid, a fluffy white feather I had found on the pavement, a small pebble from the beach where I had met my first love, and my most treasured possession.

I had owned it for nearly fifteen years. The day I had found it had been so special, and over the years that followed, the day had taken on almost magical properties. Memories can be like that. I had been staying with my Granny and Grandad, because Mum had to work, and Dad had been gone a while. It was summer, and the days were long and sunny. I was going to be twelve, and there had been talk of a cake and fizzy drinks.

The morning of that day, the postman had knocked on the door, and Granny had taken in a parcel, shaking her head at Grandad, when she found it was addressed to him. He had jumped up from the table, his toast and marmalade forgotten.

"It's here! Lucy! Come and help me open it." He had danced around the living room and into the kitchen, singing at the top of his voice. "Stop, wait a minute Mr Postman." Laughing his high-pitched giggle, and finally brought back to earth when I sat on the floor and tried to open the box.

Inside, there were sections which needed to be joined together. We sat happily with a spanner and a screwdriver, but even when it was put together, I had no more idea than when we started what it was.

Granny was clearing away the breakfast things by then, and smiled slowly. She told him to load the car, while she made us a picnic, and we set off to the beach. My Granny was probably glad of the peace. We were, however, Grandad and me, officially on an adventure. He refused to tell me what it was, and I spent the journey in the car shouting out more and more bizarre guesses. When we were with Granny, we had to be a bit calmer, but left on our own, we were loud, and silly. I miss him.

At the beach he parked the car, and we took his new and exciting thing onto the sand, he slipped the headphones onto my head and told me to listen for beeps. Immediately, he held the plate shaped end of the contraption up to my belt buckle and the beeps came loud and strong in my ears.

"It's a treasure finder!" He declared. "Any treasure on this beach is ours, Lucy!" Setting off at a good pace, so that I had to trot to keep up, he scanned the sand, backwards and forwards until we reached the cliff. "You try. There has to be some treasure here somewhere!" He handed me the handle, and I passed over the headphones. All morning we took turns scanning the sand, and listening to the beeps that never came. We stopped for lunch and found that Granny had packed pies and sandwiches, crisps and bottles of juice. "Do you think we're doing something wrong?" Grandad asked me. "I thought we would find much more treasure than this."

"Maybe it's supposed to be hard to find, otherwise, someone else would have found it?" I asked him, not sure if what I was saying made sense. He snatched me up and swung me through the air.

"Genius!" He cried as I swooped through the air. "I have a super-humanly intelligent grand-daughter." We laughed, falling onto the sand, waving our feet and arms in the air.

"We could try further down, now that the sea is further out, I suppose." He jumped up, grabbing my hand and the metal detector.

"Fantastic idea. Come on." He ran to the surf, and we listened and scanned, for another two hours. I believe that he was about to quit, when I heard the beeps.

"Grandad! It's beeping." I shouted. He scanned back again, watching my face, and then grabbed the small shovel that had been hanging from his belt all day, for just such an occasion.

He dug, and I dug. We kept going, until we found an enormous, rusty, six inch nail. He sat on the sand, clearly disappointed.

"I'm not sad that we found this. It's not just a nail, Grandad. It's a nail from a pirate ship." He took the nail that I held out to him.

"Yes. This nail has probably seen some battles at sea, and maybe even some shipwrecks." His eyes grew wide in his face. "It might have belonged to Black Beard himself."

"Best treasure ever, Grandad." I felt my hand in his, the sand rough on our skin, the salt from the water on my lips, and we walked back to the car, packing up our treasure carefully.

Twelve years later, I had reminded him of the day we searched for treasure on the beach, and we had laughed. Not so loud, and with less jumping about, but the feeling had been the same. The beeps I had listened for that day, as he closed his eyes and slipped away, had been the hospital machinery, and the treasure had been his heartbeats, which stopped. The silence had been devastating.

Today, I have another special favourite thing to add to the box, and the other treasures will, I hope, make me brave enough to do what comes next.

In the box, next to the pebble, the feather, the fake flower, and the rusty nail, now lies the white plastic wand, with two blue lines in the window. My stomach is still flat, but that will change over the next few months.

I close the lid of my box carefully, and rest my hand on the top of it. I wish my Grandad could be here to meet my baby, I hope I can be strong enough to go on this new adventure without him. The sun shines in through the window, and I remember that the summers are short, and I should go now, and walk on the sand, before the wind changes, and brings clouds and rain.

Slipping my flip flops off my feet, so that I can feel the sand, I walk the length of the beach, keeping my eyes peeled for any treasure I might find.

17.

The Face You Show

This part of town is tough. We see more police cars than florist's delivery vans, but it suits my budget for the moment, and I have learned a great deal from living here. Downstairs from my place lives Belinda, who earns her living from the passing trade, she is bright and funny, and very anti-drugs, which surprised me, because my head was filled with cliché and stereotypes. She saw me move in and carried boxes in so that nobody took my stuff from where I had left it. We have lunch once a week and we laugh until we cry. She has become my closest friend.

Upstairs from me, lives Saul, who is very quiet. You would hardly know he was there. He is always polite and replies when I say hello, but he has never started a conversation with me. That's it. We are the entire occupants of this squat, dilapidated building but we get along and pay the rent.

I know that Belinda is curious as to why I am here but she has not asked me, just as I have not asked her how and why she does what she does. Everyone here has their own secrets and mine can hide next to theirs.

I have lived here for four months patiently waiting, and watching but nothing has happened. I have watched Belinda, who puts on her tough face before she leaves the house, and Saul, who hangs his head and avoids eye contact. I have decided to try to look as though I am in a hurry to get somewhere so I never dawdle or pause. I rush and hustle myself through the streets and back to my hiding place.

My window looks out over the street and I sit in my chair,

and I watch who comes and who goes. My eyes are tired from scanning the faces of people who pass, but I have yet to see the one I am looking for.

Today is Tuesday, and I am due to have lunch with Belinda. We have ordered food from the Moroccan place around the corner because they deliver, not because the food is good. A man was attacked outside the house yesterday and he is in hospital, so we are staying close to home for a few days until it calms down.

Saul has agreed to join us, and we sit in my place and talk about nothing. The food is alright and we eat. We have a glass of wine each and the conversation is easy and comfortable, surface stuff. My eyes are drawn to the window from time to time when a noise or a shout floats up from the street.

We talk about the places we lived before this. Saul lived with a girl on the other side of the city, but she left him and he needed a place that was cheaper. Belinda used to work for a club up in the West End, high prices for the club, not so much for the girls, and she decided to work for herself. They both look at me expecting me to tell them. I start to tell the lie I have prepared about a failed marriage, but these people are my friends, and I am tired of lying.

"I used to live in the country with my husband, and my daughter. She met a man, a lot older than her, who filled her mind with dreams and her veins with drugs. She died. My husband went after the man and shouted his pain at him. The man followed my husband home, smashed down the door, and killed him. I am all that is left. I want to see the man, and I want him to see me, and face what he has done. He came out of prison three months ago and this is where he came from. I believe he will come back. I want to face him, tell him what he has done to everyone I love." I shrugged. "That's what I am waiting for."

"What makes you think he will stand still and listen?" Saul's head tipped to one side.

"I can think of nothing else to do. I had to do something. I couldn't sit in the house where they both died and do nothing." I had done enough of that.

"Who is he? We might know him." Belinda's hand was warm on mine.

I went to my kitchen drawer and pulled out the newspaper report from when it all happened. They shared it, while I made coffee. I heard the rustles of the paper and the murmurs from each of them, but in my mind, I saw the three of us, so happy and normal, before we became a newspaper story.

They had finished reading when I got back. Their faces set.

"His brother, runs the bar down the street." Belinda told me.

"I know."

"And more besides." Saul rested his hand on the table next to mine.

"I know."

"What do you want him to do?" Belinda watched me carefully.

"I want him to know. What he did to me."

"He spent time in prison, he knows. Why put yourself in danger?" Saul was talking to me, but looking at Belinda. I should never have told them, I had held it together, until now.

"It's fine, don't worry. I will probably never see him, and if I do, I don't know if I would even be able to speak to him." I shrugged, as though it was unimportant, but neither of them believed that, and neither did I. Lunch was over, and they left. I sat by my window and the dishes sat in dirty water, congealing in the sink.

What would I say if I saw him? I had no plan. They were right, I had put myself in danger with no firm idea about what I would do if he was in front of me. Stupid featured strongly in my mind.

Two days later I saw him for the first time. He was walking into the bar his brother owned. I stopped breathing for a moment. The man who had wrecked my life was in the street below my window. This was what I had waited for.

My feet carried me down the stairs. Saul was coming in and I pushed past him. I crossed the road, and met the man I had waited for. I watched him recognize me, watched confusion and surprise mix with anger. I stood in front of him and I had nothing to say.

"What?" He stepped towards me.

"I need to talk to you." His friends were clearly intrigued about why some random woman old enough to be his mother was making any effect on him. "Ten minutes, that's all. I'll buy you a coffee." I pointed to the little café on the corner, and I was surprised when he agreed.

We sat at the table with a sticky plastic cover, and I searched for the words I needed. He held his hand out, as though I was wasting his time.

"You killed my daughter and my husband. You have wrecked my life. What can I do to make you understand how dreadful what you did was?" My hands reached across the table towards him.

"I went to prison, on your word, bitch. Your daughter wanted the drugs, I didn't make her take them, she was bored of the life you gave her. Your husband was an arsehole. He thought he could shout and tell the world what was right. He started the fight. It was his fault. But I was the one who went to prison. You stood in court and told them how I was such a bad guy, but you took no responsibility for raising a drug hungry slapper, or encouraging your self-important idiot of a husband to take me on. This is your fault, as much as it's mine." His arrogance came at me in waves. I wanted to fight back, but there was nothing left inside me, I was too broken.

The waitress brought coffee, whilst I tried to work out how to explain myself. He dumped in two sugars and stirred, and I watched the liquid follow his spoon. I felt dizzy, light headed. He drank the coffee and smiled.

"I loved my daughter, and so did her father. We were so happy together. What were you even doing there?"

"Selling drugs to white bread, vanilla little girls like yours. She was a laugh but there were loads of them, and they couldn't wait to get their hands on it all." He laughed. It was a mean cruel sound. He finished the rest of his coffee in one gulp. "Shit coffee here." He said it loud so that the rest of the café could hear it, and he left. I was shaking. Sick to my stomach and so sad.

"Move." The voice was soft in my ear. "Come on." Belinda on my left and Saul on my right, they took me home.

Inside the front door, Belinda pushed me up the stairs. Her hands firm on my bony old backside. "Pack up anything with your name on it. Hurry, the cab will be here in less than five minutes. Go." She told me as we pounded up the stairs. She stopped on the landing and yelled up the stairs. "Saul. Move it." I was standing in the middle of the room unsure what I should do next. Belinda held the door open. "Come on! What have you got here with your name on it!" She was getting louder and it seemed to kick start my brain. I ran to the drawer and pulled out the newspaper cuttings and my purse. That was all there was. I threw those pieces into my bag and followed her down the stairs. Saul clattered down after us. She had us all running. I was breathless. Belinda held open the front door. A car pulled up outside the house. In my shock I allowed myself to the swept along with her intensity. "Move." We did as we were told.

"Where to?" The cab smelled of too many late nights and takeaways. The three of us piled into the back seat.

"Waterloo, please." I sat back against the seat.

"Where are we going?" Saul's eyes were huge in his face.

"You're coming home with me." I grabbed their hands and held tight, sitting between them on the back seat. The cab pulled away from the curb. We passed the pub just as the doors flew open, and a group of young man poured into the street.

On the train, we got sandwiches and tea, and I waited for them to tell me what had happened to mean we had to run. They said nothing. I looked from one to another. Belinda shrugged.

"He sold my sister drugs, got her hooked. She worked for him on the street, no money, just for the drugs. She died with a needle in her arm and infected with so many diseases she would have probably died of those if she hadn't taken too much." She wiped a tear. "I found out where she had got the drugs. I tracked him down, and I waited. Just like you did." I looked at her. A tear slipped down her cheek. "I miss her so much. She was such a pretty little thing. She was fifteen when she died." She looked at Saul.

"My girlfriend. Natasha. I told you about her. We were falling behind with the mortgage. He talked her into carrying drugs for him. The condom burst in her stomach. She died in the airport. My brother phoned me because he'd seen it on the internet. Someone filmed it and put it on Facebook. So, I know how she died. I watched it on my phone." He watched the fields go past, out of the window for a little while, and I let him.

"We had never spoken to each other about it until the other day when you told us about your daughter. Today, when you met him, you maybe didn't notice who your waitress was?" I shook my head. I had been focused on talking to him. "It was me. I brought the coffees. Saul and me, we mixed in the same amount as broke in Natasha's stomach, into his coffee. We paid him back."

"Ah that's why we had to leave?" They nodded. "Why those men were running from the bar?" They nodded some more. "When we get home. We will all need some rest and good food."

"Can we stay with you, for a little while?" Saul held my hand on the table.

"If you're not careful, I'll adopt the pair of you." Belinda put her hand on top of ours, and for the first time in the longest while, my tears were happy, not for my daughter. Not for my husband, not for loss, but for me, and for my friends. They had taught me to show the face to the world that needed to be shown, and to show my heart to those who loved me.

18.

Tickling Toes

The grass was beautiful, so lush and green, I had never noticed before, how hard each tiny plant works to push out of the soil and up towards the sun, cut down by the lawnmower, then growing again, so resilient, so strong despite what the world does to it. I could feel each blade of it on my bare feet, as I walked on the springy carpet it provided.

I have spent so much time, being something to everyone, trying to be the right sort of someone. I was a Mum, I tried hardest at that one, but, I think, still messed it up. A Daughter, I tried hard on that one too, but I never felt that what I did was good enough. A wife. I think I tried least at that one.

I stopped being a wife. I was so relieved to stop.

I carried on being a daughter, until there was nobody left to be a daughter for. I hoped that at some point one of them would say, thank you, that was nice, you have been someone we are proud of. They never would have said that, because they would not have thought it important, or perhaps, they did not feel it was earned.

I tried to be a sister. It worked to some extent. I count my sister as one of the best friends I have had in the world, and I hope she would agree. My other siblings have drifted away, without fuss or particular fury, just lack of interest on both sides, and I have let them drift down river. Glad, if I was honest, to see them go.

I am a Mum. The most wonderful thing to be. Bringing someone into the world, screaming and squealing, is a sweaty, messy business, but so worthwhile. Each day that passes, at that age brings changes, and you watch and you feel each breath in and out, and every cry and every tear. Tiny fists flail in anger, and calm, sleeping peacefully, and the feeling that you have been absolutely blessed to be allowed to have this wonderful tiny person in your life, is huge, and humbling. I imagined that this was the best time, and then, a month went by, and then a year, and each change, brought a more interesting, more amazing person into my life. The tiny person grows into an adult, one piece at a time, and you watch, with bated breath, to see what they will do, and who they will become. You think they have achieved something incredible and they go ahead and surprise you with more, and better. I have imagined, so many times that I would explode with how proud I was, and that nothing could be better, but each time I have been wrong, I did not explode, and the next thing was better than the last.

I am a wife again, second time, and it's so much better. Or am I better? Or is it just a more suited husband. I have no real understanding of how these things work, I have dithered and meandered through life with no plan or purpose.

Somehow, though, today it seemed that every moment of my life has been leading up to this. Every mistake I thought I made, has been the perfect action, because it brought me to this. I have lived a life filled with silliness, tears, laughter and love. I have good friends, some of whom I have known for nearly as long as my life. Some more recent, but no less dear to me. I have been lucky, and unlucky, in almost equal measure. I have worked hard, but not without learning from it, not just for the sake of being tired.

When all of these things are added up, it makes a life. Mine.

So why was the grass so interesting? Because today I visited a doctor and what they told me makes me appreciate how wonderful my life has been. I thought that I was nearing the end. I really believed that they would tell me that I had a limit on my dreams and on my time. I know we all do, but I thought they would give me a time, tell me to pack my bags, because I was already heading into the departure lounge. The news, however, was nothing like that. It was that I have the same chances as anyone else of being hit by a bus, and the same chance as anyone else of being here next Christmas, next birthday.

I had told nobody, I thought I would not want to worry them, until I knew for sure that I had a reason to worry, they would be angry that I shut them out, perhaps, so I cannot now share my good news, with anyone else except the grass, which keeps on growing and being as green as it can.

I decided I would celebrate anyway. I would tell my husband, he had noticed that I was worried, because he lives with me, and knows when I am being more odd than usual. Crankier, and snappy. I would tell him that I was worried, and that there was no reason. He would shake his head, and wonder why, but he would like the idea of a celebration.

So, it is not the grass that has changed, but me. I have been handed a reprieve, and I am grateful, all the way to my bare toes, finding the tickling of the grass such a wonderful experience, and wondering why I have not noticed it before.

19.

Time is on Our Side

Caroline had always loved Hapsford Manor, as a child her greatest treat was to walk through the house, and run through the gardens, imagining the lords and ladies who had walked there before her. Later, she had volunteered, and helped with the gardens, and then in the house. Her enthusiasm for the Tudor mansion was rewarded with a full-time job, in the ice cream kiosk, working her way up from there through tour guide, and finally she was the assistant manager.

She locked up every evening, making sure the building and exhibits were secure, and she was always the last to leave. Her car the last in the car park, and her smile as she locked the door, a good night to an old friend.

The weekends were the busiest times, and school holidays, but as expected, that Wednesday in October was not busy, and it was getting dark by half past four. She sent the staff and volunteers home, and walked through the house, turning off the lights, as she went. The heavy door was only used for visitors, she slipped through the side door, and looked up, surprised to see that she had left a light on at the other end of the house. Shaking her head at her own stupidity, she let herself back in and turned on the lights, making her way back through the rooms, to the room they had set up as a servant's bedroom. The light was off. She shrugged. She was tired, perhaps she had been mistaken.

The room looked different, the night clothes were left unfolded and the bed was less tidy than usual. She straightened the room and laid out the night clothes. Closing the door slowly, she walked through the kitchen, lining up the spoons on the kitchen table, so that they were straight. The long gallery was her favourite room, with leaded windows to one side, and a view across the park and the driveway. Tapestries hung along the other opposite wall, hand stitched and huge, they had always fascinated her, the hours of work, so painstaking and beautiful, still so vivid hundreds of years after they had first been made. There were repairs here and there too, where they had been damaged over the years. One, famously, had been damaged when Cromwell's army had taken the manor, and the family had pulled the tapestries out of the way to hide them, snagging one on something.

She stepped over the velvet ropes, and looked closely at the tapestry, there, in the very centre of a white flower, was a tiny group of red stitches. They stood out, and looked a little clumsy against the tiny stitches of the original. Reaching out, she touched the red stitches, running her finger across them from right to left.

A sound behind her startled her. Spinning around, the velvet rope was gone, and a man in a dark suit walked towards her, leaning heavily on a cane. She stepped away from the tapestry, watching him.

"Hello." The cut glass accent was clear in one word. "I'm not sure that I have met you before, are you the new girl?" Caroline nodded, not sure what to say. "Good. Wonderful. We need the help with all the chaps away. You land girls have been a complete joy to have here. I am here alone you see, since my wife passed away." She fell into step with him. "It's a rather wonderful place, I hope you will enjoy it here." They walked slowly, at his pace. The whole building was different, the heavy drapes were pulled tightly together, and the floors and carpets looked dusty and uncared for. "You have arrived at an opportune time. The girls are looking forward to some company. My nephew Tom will be down tonight, bringing some chums of his with him, and we have rigged up the gramophone. There will be dancing, we hope." He smiled, his deep-set brown eyes creasing at the edges.

The girls were waiting in the great hall, the wide flagstone floor would be the perfect place to dance. Caroline was introduced to Doris, Kathy, Jennifer and Theresa. They seemed friendly and excited, especially when a car pulled up outside and in bounded six men in their early twenties. It was easy to see which one was Tom, he looked like his uncle, the same warm eyes, and easy smile. Jennifer lost no time, and soon there were records playing, and they were dancing. It had been a long time since she had danced in a man's arms, and it felt rather wonderful. They all danced with everyone, and then everything stopped for tea, because it was all that was to be had. Tom brought his cup over to Caroline. His smile was easy, but his eyes were shadowed.

"I am so glad you're here with my uncle. He gets lonely rattling about in this big old place." He clinked his cup with hers. The whole thing was so strange. "Thank you for setting this up. A break from thinking about what comes next is very welcome, and I have enjoyed dancing with you, very much." He smiled down into her face. She thought, just for a moment that he might kiss her. She would not have minded. At all. He pulled away, though, and Jennifer put another record on. They danced again, and again, until her feet were hurting. The time came, for Tom and his friends to go, they loaded themselves into the truck, and waved goodbye. Tom ran his fingers down the side of her face. "I'll be back to see you, Caroline." He whispered, she reached up and touched her lips to his cheek.

"Stay safe." She whispered into his ear.

They drove away, waving and shouting, and they all went inside. The girls went to bed, but Caroline volunteered to wash up the tea things. On her own again, with too many thoughts, she pushed the cups and saucers into the cupboard, and walked through to the long gallery. Her fingers tracing the side of her cheek where his had lingered. The tapestry was waiting. The red stitches bright as berries. Caroline held her finger out in front of her, and traced the stitches left to right, keeping her eyes shut. Slowly, she opened them, and found the velvet rope was back in place, and so was she.

She turned off the lights, and locked the door, then climbed into the car. Her fingers traced the line his fingers had made, and checked that all the lights were out this time.

Knowing the history, better than any of her tour guides was not a benefit in this situation. Tom Hapsford had been in the RAF, and had been shot down, and listed as missing in action in 1944. She had spent the evening dancing with him, though, of that she was certain. A tear slipped from her eye when she pulled up at the gates, and the cold October wind blew through the trees, whipping the last of the leaves into the air. She loved this place, and always would. Of all the men she had gone out with, none had measured up to him, and he had been dead for seventy-seven years.

Her Mum was right, she spent her life living in the past, and buried in the stories, at the manor. Her foot over the brake pedal, she looked in the rear-view mirror. The light was back on. She pushed the gear stick into reverse, and turned on the driveway, driving fast back towards the house. He was waiting for her by the front door.

"Tom?" She stumbled out of the car.

"Caroline. I, came back for you, couldn't stay away." She ran into his arms, feeling the warmth of him against her. "I couldn't stop thinking about you." His hands held her face, his eyes searching hers, as his lips gently caught hers. "Say you feel the same." The wind blew across the park, chilling them both.

She would never be sorry to see the staff pack up for the evening, because that was her time with Tom, every night, they had the whole manor to themselves, and time was on their side.

20.

Tree house

When he told me that he had a surprise weekend for me, I thought he had booked a hotel, a nice meal, time to spend wandering around a town we had never visited before. I was curious.

He packed, so that I would have no clues about the surprise, and we set off early in the morning. An hour later we were still driving, and he kept me entertained with clues, none of which were actually related to where we were going. We were laughing together though, which was good. It felt good. The music was playing quietly in the car, and we were relaxed and happy.

When we pulled up in the woods, I was surprised but ready to humour him. The path that led between the trees was an easy stroll, rather than a hike, and the sounds of the forest surrounded us on all sides. The quiet was amazing, only us and the birds were talking, and then it was only the birds, as we fell silent, awed by the magnificence around us. The trees were tall and wide, and the forest floor thick with fallen leaves, and pine needles.

I think we walked about a quarter of a mile from the car, before we came to the house, a wooden cabin, build on stilts thirty feet above the forest floor. A walkway let from the ground level to a wide deck, and then to the cabin itself. We walked up, breathing in the smell of the place, the feeling of total isolation and freedom.

Inside the house was perfect, there was a kitchen a bedroom and a comfortable living room. The bathroom was small, but everything seemed to work. He produced a bottle of champagne, and glasses. We sat on the deck and sipped. I looked across at him, and we shared a smile.

We were level with the branches of the trees, able to look directly into them. I imagined what it might be like to be a bird and land on the branches. The place was magical. I told him so, and that it was a lovely surprise. He checked his phone and shrugged, there was no signal. I had not expected one, and to be honest, perhaps that was the attraction of a place like this, to be completely away from the life we thought of as normal.

I stood up, and walked to the railing, watching the woods around us, listening to the rustle of leaves and the movement of bushes as the usual residents of the forest grew used to our presence. The railing ran all the way around the house, and the views changed as I walked around.

At the front, I passed the walkway again, and stopped to lean against the railing. I heard him crossing the deck towards me. I felt his hand on my shoulder. I smiled. I actually smiled.

I saw none of this coming. Out in the middle of nothing, far away from everyone, and everything. No argument, none of the usual build up to him losing his temper.

Then I was falling, tipped over the edge. Then nothing, for a while. When I did wake up, I was surprised to find that I was still in the woods. I was alone, and wandering, searching for the car, trying to find a way back. Then I found the freshly dug ground, where my body lay, cold and dead. Where he had put me, with my neck at an impossible angle, where I would lie forever, with no way back, no route home.

I am tied to this place. There is no choice to leave. It is not such a terrible place to be. I see the seasons come and go. The birds and the small animals pass me by and rarely notice me at all. Sometimes I climb up the walkway and remember the day I sat there with him.

Other people come to the house. Couples wanting a romantic weekend away in the woods. Families with young children running through the woods, chasing each other, and building memories to take with them into their adult years.

Often, I wonder why he did it. We had our problems, but he could have walked away. I struggled with the question, until yesterday, when he arrived with another woman. He looked a little older. They talked as we used to, sat on the deck as we had, and I rushed up the walkway to warn her, to tell her to run, but she was over the edge before I reached the decking. I was too late.

She lay in the leaves, with her neck twisted just as mine had been. I watched him carry her to where I lay and he dug another hole. He pushed her in and filled in the hole. I sat, long after he had collected his belongings and loaded them back into his car. I waited, and when she woke up, I found that we had things to talk about.

Every day, we practiced, and slowly we learned to affect our surroundings, rather than drift through them. We watched the children play and the couples romance each other, until the day that he returned. Another woman climbed the walkway with him, but this time we were ready for him. He popped the cork from the champagne and poured her a glass.

She smiled and sipped, and her scream echoed around the forest as he seemingly tipped over the edge of the railing, plunging to his death. She could not see that we ran with all our power, pushed with everything we had, and dove with him to the ground, taking him headfirst into the forest floor.

A silence followed, while her screams subsided, and she ran for the car, and a phone signal. Police and ambulance services arrived, and they took his body away.

We sat, my friend and I, and enjoyed the view, as the leaves turned orange and brown around us, and we passed towards another winter in the woods.

21.

Walk me home

The main street was busy, loads of bars, and clubs, their neon signs and loud music making the pavement feel like a place for a party.

"I have to go. Sorry. I can't have another one. Night lovely. I'll call you in the morning." I hugged Sophie. She was already well on the way to being drunk, so were the rest of the accounts department. I had worked for Martingales for nearly a year now, and I really liked the people, and the work was easy enough, but these work nights out were definitely not for me. I waved to the rest of them, and made my way out of the bar and down the street.

I regretted wearing the stupid shoes that hurt my feet. They were pretty, but my toes were scrunched together and my heels were crying out to be barefoot.

The side street was so much quieter, and a good deal darker too, but the dark had never bothered me, and the quiet was good after the noise of the bar.

I heard the steps behind me, keeping pace with me, perhaps I should have been worried. I did walk a little faster, the night was cold now that I was outside, and my dress was thin against the chill of the evening air. The high buildings on both sides of the road bounced with the echo of my heels. The first drops of rain fell, fat, and cold. I had no hood and no umbrella. Swearing quietly under my breath, I shrugged. Only a few more minutes and I would be home, and I could put the stupid shoes away in their box until I had forgotten how much they hurt me.

"Julia!" The voice was familiar, and I turned to see who was calling me. He lumbered towards me, and I sighed. It was Graham, the most annoying man in the accounts department. "Why did you leave? I wanted to talk to you."

"Sorry Graham. I have to go home. I'll see you in the office on Monday." I lifted my arm to wave.

"I wanted to ask you something." He was only ten feet away now.

"Graham, it's raining, I'll see you Monday." I backed away. He moved towards me.

"I'll walk you home, we can chat on the way." He was nearly with me. The whole situation was making me uncomfortable. How many times could I say no, and be ignored by this idiot?

"Graham, no. I'm fine on my own thanks." I held my hands out in front of me to show him I wanted him to back up.

"Don't be silly Julia. I'm happy to see you home safely."

"Graham. I said no. I meant it. Please can you stop patronising me. Please stop." My hair was wet, and the rain was dripping down my back.

"Julia, you're being silly." He reached out and took hold of my arm. I could feel his fingers gripping.

"Take your hand off me." I whispered it, taking in his bulk blocking my path, his hand still gripping. His hair slicked wet against his head. He smiled, and pushed me. I let him. The bricks in the wall behind me were rough through my thin jacket, and my dress. My skin was super sensitive to the texture and the feeling of the world around me. His face was too close, and the smell of second-hand beer was too strong.

He pushed. My arm was pinned against the wall, and his smile had become something much more unpleasant. The skin on my arm was pinched between his hand and the wall, and it hurt. I considered Graham, underachieving, angry, frustrated and weak. I could have felt sorry for him, almost.

"Last chance. Take your hand off me."

"Last chance?" He laughed. "What are you going to do about it?"

"Oh baby." I cooed. "I haven't played for the longest time, and I'm hot." I wiggled my hips, threw my head back and laughed. God, it felt good. I had spent two years being the best accountant I could be. I was bored.

The first punch took him by surprise. His eyes opened wide, as he bent double, sucking breath in. His grip on my arm loosened. My knee connected with his face, a cracking noise confirming his broken nose. He sank back to sit on his heels, his face bloodied and confused.

"Yes! This is fun." I lifted my knee to the side, good grief, was he still looking up my skirt, all the time until my foot extended, and connected with his face. "For fuck's sake Graham. You are a sick bastard." He lay on the street, bleeding. A buzz zipped up through my body. This was something. This felt alive. "Go home, Graham."

My feet felt great, I danced down the street, singing and laughing. This was what I had missed. All those hours, checking figures, keeping everything in columns. Being neat. I had tried to fit myself into that world, but I was pretending. I would not be going in on Monday. I would not be Julia anymore. No more pretending.

22.

Circles in the Water

I had been waiting for days, preparing, reading and spending my time alone and letting my mind run free. I had made and wrapped everything I needed, all I needed now was the right day. No, the perfect day. It had to be crisp and cold and clear, and have the right amount of sunshine, and almost no breeze. It needed to be still.

The next day it rained, and then the wind blew, as it often did in Autumn. I spent each day watching out of the window. There was nothing else to do, I needed to keep my mind in the right space until it was time to go.

Then it was Thursday. As soon as I opened my eyes and saw the light across the ceiling of the bedroom, I felt it. Like ripples and bubbles in my belly. I pulled a dress over my head and left my feet bare, collecting the two figures I had made out of lead, shaped and modelled. The cord was wound around my wrist, red and gold cords, like the red and gold in his hair. I tied my hair up, out of my face. The strap of my bag sat steady on my shoulder. I stepped out into the cold morning air.

The ground was cold, and my feet were chilled, but that meant nothing. I was on my way. There was no wind, it was still and clear. The fluffy white clouds hung in the bright blue sky. The perfect day had arrived.

At the bank of the lake, I stopped. The water was so still that it reflected like a mirror. The autumn colours were unmoved or changed by any ripples or movement. Everything was still. I breathed, slowly, deeply, calling on every woman in my ancestry who had made the journey, made their choice, and passed the method on to their daughter, to support me.

Stepping into the shallows, feeling the mud soft between my toes, the water lapping around my ankles. My dress floated on the top of the water, and the coldness seeped into my bones, as it had for my mother and my grandmother before her.

Each step took me deeper. The water reached higher. The cold hit my thighs. The time had come. I was ready. I closed my eyes, pulling in a smooth breath, not allowing the cold to shudder my breathing, pushing the cold out of my body, replacing it with love.

The bag swung on the strap across my shoulder, and I reached inside, filling my hand with the herbs and aromatics that I had collected, ground and mixed. Closing my eyes, and breathing in the cool air, I trailed the sweet-smelling powder in a circle around me. The aroma felt like a cloud of love and joy surrounding me. When the handful ran out, I pulled out another and another, turning three times in all. Then I held my hands out to my sides and said the words. The ones I had been practicing. The rite, the chant that changed lives, and moved me into a long line of powerful women who controlled their own destiny. The tiny lead figures were heavy in my other hand.

Starting at their feet, I bound them together with the cord, wrapping around and around, slowly, my fingers keeping a constant speed and rhythm. When I had the length of my forearm left in cord, I tied the knots, that had to be tied, one, two three. Then on the other side, one, two three.

Holding the figures under the water, breaking through the surface, through the reflections, ripples spreading from my hand, towards the other side of the lake.

Wait, I heard the word in my head, I had heard it all my life, learned the ritual, learned the words, the steps to the dance my feet were still making in the soft mud.

The breeze picked up and the water moved with the wind. The world stood still, but the wind lifted my hair, rustled through the golden leaves, and rippled the water, all the way back from the other shore of the lake, until they hit my hand, and the water sucked at the two tiny figures in my hand. Slowly, with careful deliberation, I released the cord wrapped couple into the water. The water pulled them in to the depths of the lake, and the breeze dropped back to nothing.

It was done. I had completed my destiny. I had called the man I had chosen and now I had to wait. If he arrived, then he was mine for life. The water was cold, but my feet were warm. I turned slowly around.

The crack of a twig told me that I had company. There he was. His red gold hair glinting in the morning sun.

"I woke up, and the first thing I thought was that I had to come and see you. I walked past your house. I didn't even knock. I just kept walking." He shrugged. That soft, floppy haired shoulder lift he always did when he was a little unsure. "You must be freezing in that water." He held out his hand to me, and I took it.

We walked back to my place, so that I could change and get warm.

Out on the lake, a perfect circle of powder floated out to the centre, where the two figures popped up to the surface. The powder circle contracted, forming a coating over the figures, bubbles from the cord slipping into the water, as the coated figures sank to the bottom of the lake, and the soft mud, where they bumped to a halt.

The weather changed, the wind picking up leaves on its way and swirling around my house, where we were safe and warm inside.

The tiny figures in the lake stayed wrapped in the cord, and slowly as the wind whipped the water up on the top of the lake, the soft silt at the bottom slowly covered the figures little by little, until they were completely buried. The spell was cast, and now that it had been sealed, it was unbreakable.

Witchcraft had been in my family for as long as we had been a family. When the religious zealots were rushing around attacking lonely women, who liked cats and sometimes refused to sleep with the local powerful idiots, accusing them of being in league with the devil, my ancestors had quietly communed with nature, harnessing the power that lies dormant there until someone who knows the old ways unleashes it and bends it to their will. The old ways were there before the church, when we were in tune with the world and everything in it.

People forgot how to be themselves when they cloaked themselves in the new ways. They spent their lives drenched in guilt thrashing around instead of allowing the freedom that is theirs by right to flow.

I will teach my daughter the old ways, and when the time is right, she will take a walk to the water to ask her questions and receive her answers.

23.

Halloween Hot Spot

"Hurry up, come on. The gap will close, and that will be it." Maurice pushed his way through the crowd. "If that happens, we won't be able to collect the fear."

Gerald followed his friend. "Wait for me. Maurice!" The corridor was full, and he had to find his way between the other minor demons in his way. Pushing his way through the throng earned him a few pokes and pushes.

Maurice and Gerald made their way to the small gap in the veil. They had brought a ladder with them and Maurice climbed up, and put his hand through. He followed with his head. Gerald giggled. All he could see was the lower half of his friend. Remembering that time was short, he followed his friend up onto the ladder, and grabbed hold of his foot, before it disappeared too.

They both landed with a noise that was halfway between a bump and a splat. Gerald blinked his eyes. It was bright after the dim gloom of the minor demon hallways. They sat on the concrete, unsure what to do next.

"Come on Gerald." Maurice straightened his horns. "You don't want to be a minor demon for all eternity, do you?" He bustled off, his tail bouncing off the uneven pavement slabs. "This could take us to the big time, we could be up there with the best of them, well, the worst of them."

Gerald picked up his tail and tucked it over his arm. "Maurice, how are we going to do it, though? We have to really scare people. Are we up to it?"

Maurice came to a halt. The corner they had turned took them into a quiet street.

"This is perfect, Gerald. I bet we could terrify the people who live here. Look, they're so frightened of the dark, they have made little lanterns out of pumpkins. It's not even dark here, with all the other lights." Maurice laughed, his yellow teeth shining wetly.

A group of small children, and a couple of adults laughed their way up the path and knocked on the door. Maurice and Gerald couldn't believe their luck. A whole group of people they could frighten, they could catch the fear in one big bubble. The door opened and the children held out small buckets. When they turned around, Gerald and Maurice shook their hands and screamed their best blood curdling screams. The children laughed, delighted with the demon's performance. The woman from the house came down the steps and patted them both on the head, giving them each a sweetie.

Maurice's eyebrows bunched together. This was not going according to his plan. They went to the next house and the next, and each time, they were met with happiness, laughter, screams of delight.

"I don't understand Gerald. We did all the scariest stuff, best we ever did, and they laughed, they liked it. They even gave us this stuff." He thumped his fist down onto the bag of sweets he had collected. "What are we going to do? We can't go back, and tell him what happened. We'd be demoted even lower than being minor demons. We'd be splat monkeys, scraping the bottom of the pits. If we're lucky." He covered his eyes with his hands and tipped his head to lean on his knees.

"So, we have to try harder. Let's go to the next street." They pushed themselves off the pavement where they were sitting, and trudged to the corner. Three zombies ran past them, and a witch followed. They were laughing. "Maurice, they just ran past two demons, and they laughed. We are ridiculous." He kicked out at the lamppost. "They think we're a joke."

They knocked at the next door. They screamed and growled and drooled. Their eyes glowed red and fiery. The woman at the door clapped her hands and gave them a sweetie to add to their growing collection.

The evening went on, with every door, every crowd of children drawing nothing but laughter.

"You know what, Maurice?" Gerald pushed a piece of chocolate into his mouth, chewing noisily. "This is not so bad. Nobody knows we are here, right. Nobody poked me with anything pointed, or stepped on my tail for fun, not all day. People are kind here, they smile at us and they give us this, nice stuff to eat. We could, well, what I'm saying is, we could stay. I'm not in any hurry to go back. To be a minor demon, or even a major demon. Especially not to be a splat monkey."

"I get what you're saying." Gerald sniffed a marshmallow and bit into it. "It might be a little different to what we're used to, but we could learn to live like this. It has been nice not having anyone hit my toes with hammers. Yes. We could just stay here, and eat this fluffy stuff." He smiled. His teeth yellow and pointed.

The street was dark, but not as dark as they were used to. They pushed themselves off the edge of the pavement, and started down the road.

"Strange how that part of the road looks different to the rest." Gerald pointed to the wet looking tarmac ahead of them. They watched the black road began to bubble, and split.

The chief of the major demons rose from the road, towering above them and the houses on either side of the road.

His voice was dark and deep as the pits of hell. "Fools. You chose the only day of the year when you could fit in around here. You are an embarrassment to demons everywhere." He flexed his giant red muscles. "Worried that you'll be splat monkeys? That's not about to happen." He rubbed his hands together and threw a ball of energy at them, evaporating them where they stood. All that remained was a sticky stain on the tarmac and the smell of roasting marshmallows.

The chief of the major demons slipped slowly back to where he belonged, as the clock towers around the town rang out the midnight chimes, and Halloween was over for another year.

24.

Prisoner of the Pills

The first of the day's light brightened the edges of the window. She had watched for most of the night, through the darkest hours. The new pills had knocked her sleep pattern completely out of step. The nights were long, and her attention span was short. Depression made it hard for her to concentrate on a film, or a book. She pushed with her hands against the arms of the chair, her body seized up after sitting for so many hours.

The window was mottled with grime. So much had changed since her dad had passed away. She had spent his last seven months caring for him, making sure he was in no pain. They had lived together, the house had sparkled, it was so clean. That was, she reminded herself, two years ago. Had she cleaned the windows since then? She ran a finger across the glass, and checked her grimy fingertip. No. She shrugged. Nobody visited. Who cared about the windows? She used to, whether visitors came or not.

The garden on the other side of the glass, once so neat and tidy, was choked with weeds, scrubby grass and overgrown shrubs. Her Dad would not have approved. A breath huffed out of her. What if she went outside? Into the garden, and maybe tidied up a little, would that be good idea? Panic fluttered in her chest, and kept her hand an inch away from the door handle.

A cup of tea, and her new shiny pills quieted the panic, so that it was in the background, not standing between her and the door.

The lock moved after a little pressure, and the light spilled into the house. She watched the shape it made on the floor, carefully stepping into the light, and feeling the warmth on her feet. Two small steps and she was on the path outside. Scuffing her slippers across the weeds helped but more was needed.

She followed the path to the shed, where her dad had hidden when she was a child, staying out of the way while her Mum fussed and worried. The tools were propped against the wall, the smell was still here, the one she remembered from back when her dad was there. There was a little rust of on blades of the clippers, and the shovel, but they would probably still work. Reaching into the shed she pulled out a fork and the old basket her dad had used to collect weeds. She would try for a little while and see if she could do it.

The new pills blurred the edges, the doctor had given them to her after her dad had passed away. 'To help you through the grief.' That had made her laugh. She had been relieved when he took his last breath. Glad to no longer have his controlling demands, and for the bruises to fade.

Now that he was not there to demand. There was no reason to clean or dig the garden. Unless, perhaps, she might do it for herself.

When was it, she pulled out the tools, while she rolled the ideas through her mind? When did she stop doing things for herself, putting herself first?

When her Mum died, perhaps, when all the slaps became hers, and hers alone? Maybe before that when she listened to her mum's tears, through the bedroom wall. Who knows how it starts?

It took all morning to take out the weeds, and make the

garden back into the tidy space it used to be. The shrubs which had survived her neglect looked better without choking weeds wrapping around them. It was more physical work than she had done in a long time, and although her muscles ached, and she was hot and tired, it felt good.

It had been a long time since she had enjoyed food, but the sandwich she made for her lunch tasted wonderful. More pills to take, to keep her lunch company, and a cup of tea. The afternoon brought shiny windows and clean carpets, and a bathroom that made her want to sink into the hot water in the bath and soak her aching body,

The garden waited for her in the dusk, just as she had known it would. The bath had been wonderful, and the house looked more like her home. Carrying the secret for two years had made her tired, and had stopped her from doing anything else. She could see it clearly now. She had been serving a self-imposed prison term, and had finally been released. Her guilt had closed the door each day, and her terror of discovery had turned the key.

Pulling the bag from her pocket, she dug a hole in the garden, as far away from the house as it was possible to go, and emptied its contents. The light was fading. It had been a productive day, and the last pieces of the light, before the dark really took over, reflected off the shiny coating on the pills. The outer casing that made sure they released their contents once they dissolved in the stomach.

The pills she had been taking had numbed the feelings that ran screaming around her brain. The guilt, the anger, the despair. The pills she had buried were the things that had made her feel so guilty. The anger was what made her give them to him, even though they were not prescribed for him. They had been given to her mother, when the pain had been beyond anything else. She had kept them, for no better reason than that she had forgotten they were there. Until the morning when he had hit her across the face, and told her that she had always been worthless, and that he had always hated her. He had spat at her. She had felt it land on her cheek.

Later in the day while clearing out a drawer, she had come across the pills, and it had felt as though her Mum was suggesting something that would help. That night she slipped him one extra pill, and he went to sleep. No shouting, no shoving. It was wonderful, and it gave her hope, that she could maybe have the peace permanently.

She replaced each of his pills with one of her Mum's ones, and he took them, still groggy from the pill the day before. She watched his breathing slow. The smile that lifted her mouth was for her and for her Mum, and for the peace and quiet.

The doctors told her how sorry they were, and she pretended to be sad. They took him away and very quickly she was able to have him cremated. Perhaps she was in shock, or denial, or both. She had been lost since then. Guilty of murder. Angry that she had been pushed to it, and grief, that she had no proper relationship with her father, and now it was too late to be repaired. There was no chance that he could realize how bad he had been as a parent, and how much he had hurt her.

These were the last of the pills she had found in her Mum's drawer. She pushed the soil over the top of them, and wondered what they might grow. A chuckle filled her throat. She had kept them, against the possibility that she might want to stop herself from breathing too. She had decided against it.

Apart from anything else, she wanted to see what the garden would look like in the Spring.

25.

Harvey's Last Ride

My eyes were stuck together, and that humming noise was back again, making my head feel like there was a bee buzzing inside my brain. It was dark, and there was a smell, a bad one. I wanted to close my eyes again. That tired, drifting feeling was back. I felt my breathing getting more regular, more even. That slipping, comforting feeling taking me down again. The noise changed, making me pay attention. I was moving.

My eyes were properly open again. This was very strange. I was moving, but it was dark, and I was squashed, my legs couldn't straighten. My hair was caught on something too. I twisted my head to the left, and my hair tugged. My neck was tight. My shoulders were uncomfortable too, like I had been squashed into a space that was too small. I pushed my hand into my hair to push it out of my face, trying make myself think more clearly. My head was sticky, my hair felt like one big lump. I felt my nose wrinkle up.

The buzzing noise started up again. There was a clicking noise too. My head still felt like it was full of cotton wool. A light filled the space, then went off again. In the seconds it was on, I discovered three things. I was in a box. There were painted metal pieces at the edges. I was not alone.

Out of the three things, the one that worried the most was the last one. My eyes had been shocked when the light went on, but the thing that registered very quickly was that lying next to me, and not breathing, even a little bit, was Harvey. He had been bleeding, not recently, but that was why my head was sticky. My hands were shaking. Truthfully, I had never liked Harvey, but I would not have wished this on him. He had a hole in his neck, and his eyes were glassy and unfocused. I felt sick, because of what I had seen, because without knowing how, I was in a box with dead Harvey, and I could see metal bits, which had been painted dark green.

Though I racked my brains, I could not imagine how I had ended up here. Trying to focus on how I had arrived there, helped me not to think about Harvey, who was taking up more than his share of the box. I screwed up my eyes really tightly, and waited to see if it would be gone when I opened them. It was dark, and Harvey was still squashed up next to me. The humming noise stopped, and we were no longer moving.

Was this good news? Perhaps someone was coming to rescue me from Harvey's sticky embrace. Or maybe the person who made holes in Harvey was planning on doing the same to me. My head was foggy again. I pushed my hand up to my head and pulled my hair out from under Harvey's face. Swallowing hard to stop myself from being ill.

Under my head was something hard, which I pulled and wiggled to free, lifting my head and pulling again. Swearing quietly each time my hand slipped, and finally dragging out a cross shaped piece of metal, which I guessed, from touch alone, was used for changing a wheel on a car. I ran my hand across the top of the box, over my head and felt the curve, and the feel of it, then followed the curve down, to find that there was a straight section. I was in the boot of a car. How had I thought it was a box? I blinked my eyes. I had been stupid. More than stupid.

There was more noise. A deep thud, shaking everything. I lay still, with the metal cross on my chest, like a buried medieval king. My only, truly one and only chance, if the person about to open the boot was not friendly, was that they would expect me to be unconscious.

The key slid into the lock, I heard it click. My stomach clenched.

I braced myself, the light would be stunning for a moment. Each breath was shallower, and quicker than the last.

The click of it opening, could have been a starting pistol, sending me out into the air, like I was on springs, my metal cross in front of me, my body weight and the solid metal cross propelled across the distance between us. Carrying him with me ending up flat on his back, with me on the grass next to him. I knew who he was.

"You fucker." I brought the cross down onto his head, flipping myself over, to straddle him. "You put me in a boot with fucking Harvey." The steel was red, in places. His blood, maybe Harvey's too. The face I had known so well, smashed.

Slowly, with lots of heaving and pushing, I lifted my ex-husband into the boot with Harvey. For a while, I hunted for the keys on the ground in the dark, until I started thinking, and realized that the keys would still be in the lock of the boot.

I recognized where we were, he was so predictable, but at least I knew how to get where I needed to go. The keys slid easily into the ignition and I drove through empty roads. It was very dark, but there was no way I would use the headlights.

The banging from the back of the car started a few minutes later, but we were nearly where I wanted to be.

The old quarry was peaceful, there was nobody about, and it was easy to drive up to the top, and turn off the engine, taking my foot off the brake pedal as I slipped from the door, and watching the car, with the banging still coming from the boot roll quietly towards the edge, picking up a little speed on the way. The descent, the last thirty feet of the journey was silent, graceful, and left me a smile.

The walk back to the road took me until the sun came up, but I was in no hurry. The morning was cool, and it was good to be outside after so long locked inside a small space. Every blade of grass, every song of the birds as they left their roosts for the morning sun took me another step away from the stupid fucker who thought he could own me then, and had tried again.

"Hey! Psycho!" I turned on my heel, and saw him coming towards me. His face was black and blue. He was bone dry. I felt my face crumple up in confusion. "I was sitting in the back seat, when you got out. Did you not hear the banging? I was kicking the back seat out. Thanks for getting rid of Harvey though." He smiled that smile that made me want to stab him. I walked away. He walked next to me. "May as well keep you company." I smashed my hand out sideways. It should have hurt him. It certainly should have connected.

"No. not going to happen. You're stuck with me, for all eternity." My hand slipped through him. I sat down on the grass at the side of the road. "We are going to have so much fun." He smiled, and I wanted, with all the violence in my soul, to hurt him more.

26.

A Life Worth Living

The house stood on the hill, high enough that you could see across the valley, and all the way to the hills beyond. They had lived in the house for more than ten years, and had been happy there. The place had been a wreck, but they had fixed it, they had done it together, and it had been fun most of the time. The house had been a home, one that both of their children had felt safe to come home to, even though they were fully grown, and had homes of their own. It had been the perfect place. The village that surrounded them was filled with friends and they had been involved almost from the start in committees and parties and always a great deal of cake and tea.

The morning that they had left the house, in plenty of time to get to the appointment, they had expected to be back home before lunchtime, with very little changed. The town had been busy, and the car park was pretty full, but they had found a space and walked back, still leaving themselves time to be early and wait.

Old friends had been sitting outside a café drinking coffee and had invited them to sit down, but they had pressed on, promising to arrange to meet them another day.

The doctor had been kind, but absolutely clear. There was no room for hope or treatment. There was no reprieve. It would be quick, and could be managed so that there would be no pain, but it would come. Soon. They drove home in silence, taking in the news. It would change everything, for ever.

For days they walked around the house, avoiding looking at each other, or talking if they possibly could, until they could bear it no more.

"I made coffee. We need to talk about this. It's happening to both of us. One of us has to go, and the other will be left alone, so we need to deal with it. We have a couple of choices, as far as I can see. We can sit here and wait for it to come, or we can have the best three months we've ever had. Go on holiday, have the kids down, whatever we want to do. Eat what we fancy, drink too much wine." Her eyes sparkled. She was the woman he had met, and fell in love with, except this was better, he knew she was his, for as long as they had.

There and then, the decision was made, they got in the car and drove to the beach, sitting on the sand and eating ice creams, while she phoned to invite the children to visit. They decided not to tell people, there would be time for that when it was necessary, and they wanted not to deal with other people's pity or concern, it would be a waste of the time they had left. It was selfish perhaps, but after a lifetime of being generous and caring, supporting others, they were due a little time to themselves.

They stayed on the beach until the sun set, and then on into the darkness. Some kids who were younger than their own arrived and played softly on a guitar, a girl was singing softly. They smiled at the old couple who danced on the sand, and held each other close. She rested her head on his chest and remembered the dances they'd had together over the years.

It was after midnight when they got home. It had been years since they were home so late. They ate a late breakfast, and sat in the garden reading the papers, and refilling their coffee cups. Online, they booked a holiday, and left the next day, sitting on a beach each day, eating food they would normally avoid, and drinking too much wine.

After two weeks they came home and welcomed their friends to the house, throwing a party for the whole village. The music played on through the evening, and into the night, and when everyone else had left, they danced together once again, her head on his chest, and their arms wrapped around each other.

"I'll miss you." They told each other. "I'll miss this."

The children came to visit, and each of them remarked how happy they found them. How contented. The visits went well, and food and wine were consumed. They were genuinely happy times.

A month went by, and then two. They realized that being happy and enjoying themselves had been a skill they had allowed to rust from lack of use. Life had got in the way, and now that they had been threatened with the loss of it, they had found the way back to living for fun.

Friends commented that they had never known them to be happier. They laughed and joked their way through the days. Every two weeks they visited the doctor for blood tests and chatted their way through them, treating themselves to a picnic on the way home.

After three months, the results that came back from the blood tests were bad. They had known it was coming, and were surprised that it made no difference. They shrugged their shoulders at the doctor and went to meet some friends for dinner.

The following week, they went to the hospital, and discussed pain relief. The days were counting down, falling through their fingers, but they carried on. The pills, then injections, kept the pain at bay, and the wine helped.

A friend invited them out for a day on his boat, and they jumped at the chance. They loved it, enjoyed the sun glinting off the water, and the feel of the wind in their faces as they rushed across the waves towards the land.

The next day they had an appointment at the hospital, and the news was bad. The painkillers were increased, and now that one of them had to stay on the ward, while the other went home, there was to be no more wine. Pain relief became a drowsy sleep, which slipped into a slow goodbye.

The children came again, with tears, and grief in their eyes.

The last day came, and he slipped away, peacefully and she thought there was the ghost of a smile on his face. Her kisses sent him safely on.

The children came again to pay respects, along with friends, and then they left, and she sat alone in the house where they had been so happy, where they had laughed, and she cried all the tears that there were in the world to cry.

They had lived and loved every second. She had grieved for him with all of her, and now she had to find the courage to live a life alone.

She pulled on her gardening gloves, and went outside. The weeds had enjoyed the time they had been ignored. She would start with them, and see what she would do next.

If she had learned one thing, it was that life was to be lived, and that a life worth living had to be one that was full and lived with love.

27.

A Walk on the Beach

The air inside the car, even with the windows open, was hot and sticky. The road ran alongside the beach for over a mile, and the breeze whipped in through the windows, the smell was intoxicating, and, although I fought my own wishes, I lost. I parked the car, and locked the doors, knowing it would be hotter than an oven when I came back to it. The sea called to me, and I was powerless to resist. It had always been that way for me.

The sun was high in the sky, and warm. I walked away from the road, and onto the beach. There was a crunch of small stones under my shoes as I slipped and slid making my way across to the sand. I was walking slowly, because I was in no rush, and also because walking on the stones was difficult.

Slowly, I made my way, and found a place where I was happy, spreading my jacket on the stones and sitting down. I watched the rhythmic roll of the waves onto the sand ahead of me. I felt soothed by the break and pull back of the water. The worries I had brought with me, washed out to sea, carried with the froth and foam back into the blue and green.

I pulled off my shoes, and tucked my socks inside them. Leaving them with my jacket, on the deserted beach. I walked to the water, and let the cold water chill the skin of my feet, and it was wonderful. Each wave that hit the beach and rinsed my feet, made me feel better.

The day had been one of the hardest I had every known. Watching my mother breathe her last had been hard. Realizing that my father had no clue that the woman who had loved him for nearly fifty years was gone, or who she was. He had no idea who I was either, but that mattered less. I had left him, that afternoon, in the gentle care of a nursing home who promised he would be fine. I walked away and heard him ask the nurse who I was. The tears were dry on my face, the skin tight where they had been.

The waves I watched had come across the world, maybe they had once flowed in a river, lapped against icebergs, and the white sanded African beaches. Whales and dolphins had been swimming in it, and now it had washed over my feet. My smallness in the world, my insignificance in the face of the global enormity that now washed my feet was brought home to me, with each cold bubbling wave.

In the shallows I watched tiny fishes which chased each other. How long did they spend with their offspring, would they recognize each other if they swam past each other in the sea? Perhaps we were not so different. The cold of the sea splashed up my legs. It was time to go. The sea, and the beach had calmed me, as I had known it would. I would recover, and be stronger. Mourning my mother would take time, and I would allow myself the time I needed. I would visit my father, and mourn him a little at a time.

Watching the sea, I thought about earlier times, when my parents had been vibrant busy people, my father had stood with me on a beach very like the one I was on, I had been sullen, teenaged and refusing to meet his eye. "If you don't stand for something Frankie, you'll fall for anything." I knew it was a longer conversation than that, but I had forgotten everything else about it. Everybody has to make a stand somewhere, to believe in something. I had been drifting, I knew it. Perhaps this was where I made a stand. This was my time to be a grown up, and take care of the man who had raised me. There were other areas in my life where I should stand up too. Maybe now was the time. Perhaps I was ready to make changes in areas of my life I had not even considered before.

I walked back, my feet covered in sand, and waited for them to dry. I brushed the sand off, and pushed them back into my socks, and my shoes. The salt in the air, dried the tears I cried, thinking about the day that had passed, and the changes that had happened in me.

The car was as hot as I had thought it would be. Opening the doors and windows allowed the breeze through. The seats were still too hot to sit on, and the air conditioning had last worked the summer before. The air was even too hot to breathe, but I did. The seats were still too hot, but I sat on them, and my shirt stuck to my back. I drove, to push a breeze through the car, and to make myself feel in control of something.

Later when I got home, and took my socks off, some sand fell onto the floor, and I smiled, cleaning it up. I had brought back more than sand with me. I had brought back the sense of peace, and the feeling that the sea connected me to the rest of the world, and that feeling is the one that stayed with me.

28.

Friends for Life

"Gillian, please, can you take this seriously." Diane tapped her hand on the table. The sun shone through the high windows, and made patterns across the wooden floor. Her eyebrows crowded together in the limited space between them.

"Diane. I am taking it seriously, I brought wine. Very serious wine. If I was not taking this meeting seriously, I would have brought vodka. Now!" She imitated Diane's table tap. "What's the next item on the agenda?"

"I am chairing this meeting, thank you Gillian." Diane was red in the face. Gillian held out her hand, allowing her to continue. Meanwhile, she passed out glasses and poured wine for the four of them gathered around the table.

Diane pulled a face and pushed her glass away. The other three sipped and smiled.

"Now, let us continue, please. The damage to the floor, needs to be repaired, and the gutters need to be looked at. I suggest that we ask Mr Holden to quote for the work, and book it in as soon as possible." Diane lifted her pen to make some notes.

"I think we should at least get a few quotes, Diane." Gillian sipped. "What does the rest of the committee think?"

"It might be an idea, Diane." Marie smiled hopefully but crumpled under Diane's scrutiny.

Scratching her notes, to do exactly as she pleased, Diane breathed heavily through her nose.

After that, they all gave up, and the meeting followed the usual route. Diane suggested, decided, noted, and moved on, there was no need for any of the rest of them to be present.

The meeting closed, and the chairs and tables put back against the wall, Gillian grabbed the now empty bottle and the glasses, slipping them into her bag.

"I really don't know why you bother coming to the meetings any more, Gillian." Diane huffed her way to the door, holding it open for Tina and Marie. She waved Gillian through, trying to hurry her.

"I don't know why any of us do. You just do whatever you think and ignore everyone else. By the way, we all know that you've got the hots for Derek Holden." Gillian giggled. "Come on Diane, relax, I know you're cross with me, but we could do so much more with the hall, if we worked together."

"Hmmmm." Diane glared her displeasure, and stomped away up the hill.

"Gillian, you're going to have to stop annoying her." Marie linked her arm through Gillian's.

"Yes, you really should." Tina linked through Gillian's other arm. Together, they walked back to Gillian's kitchen, where fresh biscuits, cake and another bottle of wine waited. An afternoon of gossip, and laughter lay ahead, in the warm homely, not very tidy kitchen. Gillian loved to cook, she adored having friends there, and spending time with her family when they had time to visit. She had lived alone for the last six years, since her husband had left, without warning or any contact in the years that followed. If she drank a little too much, and she probably did, it was understandable. Nobody judged her too harshly, with the possible exception of Diane.

Later, when the girls had gone home, and the empty bottles were out in the recycling box, Gillian decided to make some cookies, her supply was low. Tina was partial to a cookie or five. She spooned the ingredients into the bowl, and mixed, the oven hummed, and she pulled a jar of peanut butter out to add some flavour, dropping fat dollops into the mixture, then licking the spoon before throwing it into the sink.

"Still eating peanut butter with a spoon?" The voice in her kitchen made her jump.

"What?" Gillian stared across the kitchen. He was six years older than the last time she had seen him, a little greyer around the edges, but basically the same man. "What are you doing here?"

"I wanted to see you Gilly." He reached forward and held onto the back of the chair where Marie had spent the afternoon.

"So you just popped in? You didn't think of letting me know where you were for the last six years?" She swiped a tear with the back of her hand. "I worried. For ages I waited for a knock on the door to tell me you were dead. I couldn't understand why you left."

"I was depressed. I'm sorry, I was lost, unhappy, I couldn't think. I felt like I was tied in knots. I couldn't talk to you. I would have gone completely off the edge if I didn't get away when I did. I tried to explain, but I was too knotted, so I went away to get myself better." He spread his hands.

"You're just back, like you went out for a few hours, and came home. You didn't even let me know you were OK. What the fuck was I supposed to think?" She slid into a chair, crumpling her cloth into her face, her tears hot behind her eyes. "It's so completely selfish."

"I know. I know. I'm sorry." He pulled out a chair. "Is it OK to sit down?"

"No. None of this is OK. You disappeared, and the kids were

shattered by it. They were in bits. I know they aren't kids, and they had already left home, but they were so worried." She rolled her eyes. "For heavens' sake sit down, and tell me what happened." He slid the chair out, and slipped between it and the table.

"I can't."

"You can't what?"

"I can't tell you what happened. I've been ill, Gilly. I had a sort of, breakdown. I was in a hospital for a while, and then in a support unit. I've been poorly, but I don't remember much about it." He shifted his weight. "Perhaps this was a mistake. I just woke up yesterday, and I wanted to see you. To apologise, to let you know that I was alright again. I missed you." He studied his hands on the table.

"What do you want me to do?" She pushed her hair back, and filled the kettle. She shook a cup at him and he nodded.

"I don't know. I thought you might like to know. That I was alive." The kettle clicked and she poured the water into the cups and stirred, passing him the cup.

"I did. I do. I want to. I miss you. I have been so angry, worried, and frightened for you, and for me." She stirred the milk in, and put a cup on the table. It felt so intimate, she wanted to cry. "I used to wake up in the night, and imagine you lying dead in a ditch, slowly rotting. The truth is, though, that you have been away for six years, and you only thought to get in touch yesterday. I've had to endure the pity of the whole damn village. I've had to keep the pain locked away, so that the children would get on with their lives instead of watching over me. Worst of all, I've had to face the fact that either you just didn't love me enough to tell me, contact me, or you were dead. I had no idea which was worse, until you walked in here." Tears ran unchecked down her face. "You have hurt me so much."

"Gilly." He reached out and took a sip from the cup. "I am so sorry. I'm better now, I feel stronger. I am strong enough to come home, if you'll have me." He carefully put his cup on the table, conscious perhaps that she needed time to think about what he had said.

"People would laugh at me. I have a little tiny bit of pride left." She wrapped her hands around the cup as if she needed the heat.

"That might be true. You're strong. You can get past that. Or you can't. Your choice." He watched her eyes.

"What made you go. You have to tell me that." Her voice was flat.

"That morning, we had toast for breakfast. You put marmalade, jam and honey on the table, and I looked at the choice. I really couldn't work out what I wanted, and then, I thought about all the other choices. Did I want tea or coffee, did I want to do something in the garden, did I want to be here anymore? Did I like my job? My life?" He sipped again. "I just started to think about all of the things in my life. It had been bubbling a while. I went for a walk, and I just kept walking, I caught a bus, and then a train, and kept going. I felt so free, as though I had left behind all the problems, but I knew I hadn't. I didn't sleep for days. In the end, I had a bit of a melt down and I was taken to hospital." He looked around the room. "You painted the walls."

"Twice. It's been a long time." Her fingers curled, scrunching the tea towel.

"I know. I'm asking a lot. Is it too much?" He met her eyes across the table.

For a few minutes they sat, listening to the clock ticking, and sipping their drinks. She ran through all the reasons she should tell him to go, and then she ran through all the times that she had sat at the table and cried, worried, missed him. He sat, solid, and patient, while she thought it through.

"Let's give it three months, and see whether you want to stay? Or whether I want you to go." She pushed the cookie jar towards him.

"I get a cookie?" He smiled at her, and she remembered how much she had missed his smile.

"I missed you." She whispered.

"So, I can have two cookies?" He laughed. "I missed you too."

"You keep smiling like that, you can have more than a cookie." She laughed.

"Darling girl. You always had the biggest heart. I don't know how I could have been so stupid as to walk away from you. I'm so sorry." His face crumpled. "You were always my best friend."

"No. Let's not play that game. Let's start again. Ask me out." She raised an eyebrow at him.

"What?" His eyebrows crumpled into each other.

"You want another chance?" He nodded. "Then start from the start. Before we had bills and kids, and responsibilities. Let's just be us." She set her jaw, and waited.

"Gilly?" She nodded. "Are you doing anything tomorrow?"

"No." Her eyes and her heart reached out to him, could she do this, or was it perhaps a step too far?

"Would you come out with me, for a picnic?" He watched her carefully.

"That would be very nice. Thank you." She smiled carefully. "Lunchtime?"

"Yes. Oh, and one other thing." He looked straight at her. She raised an eyebrow. "Can you bring a picnic?"

She laughed, longer and harder than she had for a long time. She had missed him. He had always been able to make her laugh, even when things were tough. Could she make this step? Diane would be condescending, hit her with some rubbish about self-worth or something. Diane could, she decided, go jump. A picnic was exactly what she wanted.

"I'll bring the picnic. Where are you staying?" She watched him consider the question. His eyes did a half roll.

"In my car." He smiled, a little.

"Couch?" She offered.

"Thanks Gilly. More than I deserve." He ran a hand over his face. His features sagged with tiredness.

"Very true." She agreed. She smiled to soften her words. He met her smile with one of his own. There was a moment, a heartbeat, the air reverberated with it between them. She nodded. A tiny movement, but it was enough. He had a chance, and that was all he had ever wanted.

29.

Happy Halloween

There was a chill in the air, Autumn had arrived, swirling leaves from the trees and lifting the smell of the soil towards me as I walked past the church. Somewhere in the back of my head, I thought about what made up that smell, and wondered what proportion of it was the bodies buried there. It was an uneasy sort of thought, which rattled around, waiting for me to push it into the box where things I chose to ignore stayed. I had been haunted for years by my fear. This time of year brought the feelings to the surface. The way I felt paralyzed me.

The kids at the school where I taught were already excited about Halloween and the fun they would have and the sweeties they would eat. There was a wildness, a reckless abandon that came with Halloween which had always made me edgy until the holiday was over. I had hidden at home when I was a child, refusing to go out with the others. It had been a source of terror which I had mastered, as I controlled most things in my life, by pretending that I did not see them, or know that they were there.

The late afternoon gathered into dusk around me as I reached the high street, and breathed a little easier once the street lamps and the lights from the shops were in sight. Only one more day until Halloween. Pumpkins and witches on broomsticks were in every window. Even the cakes in the bakery had sticky orange icing, and chocolate spiders' webs. I shuddered at the thought of eating anything so disgusting.

I was finally home, fumbling with the keys to open my door, and throw myself into my house and slip the lock to keep me safe within. My stomach was tied in knots, there was no way I would be able to eat dinner, but a cup of tea might help. I was grateful to sit in the warmth of my small living room, and sip from my cup. If I could get through tomorrow at school without a complete meltdown, I could get home, turn off the lights and pretend to be out. It would be over for another year.

The morning was beautiful, cold but crisp, as I walked to school. I threw the lights on in the classroom, and breathed slowly to control the panic that the pictures on my wall threatened. Witches and werewolves were plastered across the orange paper on the pin boards. The head teacher had laughingly suggested that the children be allowed to come to school in fancy dress. I fully expected to be teaching a group of vampires and demons all day.

At nine they streamed into the class, dripping fake blood, and barely suppressed excitement. I painted on my equally fake smile, and took them through English, stories about Halloween, Maths, if I take seventeen pumpkins away from thirty, how many do I have left? Art, pictures of your favourite ghost of ghoul. Playtime saw them scream around on the tarmac, terrifying each other. At three thirty I was hugely relieved to send them home. All I had to do was to get to my house, without any further incident, and it would be over for another year.

I avoided the church, and therefore the graveyard. I walked for ten minutes longer, to stay on the main road. Finally, I opened my door, and slipped the bolt. Sitting in my house, with the curtains closed, and the warmth of a blanket wrapped around me, I felt a little better. Slowly my breathing returned to normal. I was even able to drink a cup of tea, and have half a piece of toast. It was so close to being over.

The banging on the door started before six, and I tucked the blanket a little closer around me, closing my eyes and my ears to the dread that filled my stomach. Staying quiet and hoping they would give up. The banging carried on, I felt it had been hours, my head below the blanket in the darkness. My breathing restricted by the soft fabric. My chest heaving in and out, the panic restricting my lungs with every gulp of air.

The banging became louder, and was accompanied by screams and shouts. It was nearly nine thirty when the banging stopped. I peeked out into the room, and sat up, a little less hunched. I had survived another year. Another Halloween. Time for a bath, and an early night.

Out in the hallway, I was surprised by a blast of cold air, the front door hung open. I had slipped the lock, I knew I had. The front door leaned against the wall. I heard my own gasp, as I sucked a gulp of air in.

A creak on the stairs sent me towards the front door, moving fast and holding the wall on my way. At the door, I was met by a witch, green-faced, and cackling. Behind me on the stairs when I looked behind me was a zombie, walking slowly, grunting. I drowned in my own screams. My eyes shut tightly.

Opening my eyes, just a crack, I saw a black cloaked and hooded figure. He stood tall, filling the doorway. My panic stilled. My breathing calmed. This was surely someone come to save me. I pushed myself up against the wall, leaning heavily against the paint that I had chosen, and feeling the softness of the carpet I had paid for. It would all be alright now.

"Thank you." I whispered to my saviour. "Who are you?"

The cloaked figure turned towards me, his eyes glowing red within the hood. His hands held a razor-sharp scythe. His shoulders lifted in breath.

"I, am death." His voice croaked with lack of use.

I shuffled back towards the stairs, the screaming and the panic returning. My heart beating faster than could possibly be safe. My breathing shallow and fast. On the stairs stood the zombie, his mouth wide and dribbling with blood.

"No. Please no." I heard myself screaming. That was the last I remembered. My heart gave out, I suspect. I stepped away from the heap I had become on the floor. Death nodded his hooded head at me, and scooped me up, really quite gently into his arms. To be completely honest, it was a relief. I could not have stood it a moment longer. We left through the front door, and floated past the shops, and the church, even the school where I had worked.

The streets were still filled with people, and. If they saw us, they did not show it. Perhaps they thought we were celebrating Halloween, rather than celebrating a release from fear, and horror.

The night was dark, and for once, I felt safe in the darkness.

Happy Halloween.

30.

The Little Red Sports Car

I was lucky, as a child. I could have been lonely, I suppose. My Mum was on her own, and she had to work hard, long hours, to pay the bills for us, but my Grandparents helped. They were amazing. My Grandma was a gentle soul, warm and comfortable. My Grandpa was fun. He made me laugh, until I screamed. He played long complicated games with me, driving little toy cars around the living room carpet, making all the vroom noises I could wish for, the loudest noises saved for the little red sports car, which he said was the fastest. Later, when the games were over, and we had eaten, I would sit on his knee and he would read me stories, or we would talk. I would promise him that one day, I would get a good job and buy a little red sports car, to take him to the seaside. I could see it clearly in my head even then, pulling up outside their house, and driving to the sea, the top down, and the wind blowing against us.

Every day after school I went to their house, until Mum finished work, and as I got older, I did my homework there, and waited for him to come home. Grandma baked cakes and cookies and they were delicious, I loved her, but Grandpa was my hero.

When I grew up a little, and I could have gone home on my own, I chose to keep going to their house. I no longer sat on his knee but we still dreamed together, and laughed. He pushed me to work hard at school, get the grades. The possibility of the little red sports car I still wanted dangled before me pushing me onwards. Each year he waited with growing excitement to see my report, to see how well I had done. Every year we celebrated together. I worked hard to make him proud, and I think I did. I did well in the exams, and, the summer that I was eighteen, after I passed my driving test, we went car shopping. We bought a little red sports car, which had seen better days, and spent the long months before I went to University, fixing, refurbishing, sometimes having to build parts which were no longer in production. By the time I was ready to drive away, it was a shiny red, soft top sports car, and I loved it. I was close to home still, and came home often, pulling up outside the house, as I had dreamed when I was a child. A few times I took him to the seaside in the car, and we sat on a bench and ate steaming hot fish and chips from the paper, and laughed together at the seagulls, and the way the beach huts tilted at an angle. He made me feel ten feet tall. I know now, looking back, that I could feel that tall because I stood on his shoulders.

I got the job, the one I wanted, the one with the big salary, and I helped to make their retirement easier. I bought a house for my Mum, and paid her bills so that she could stop work, and when she was ill, it was Grandpa who sat with me beside her hospital bed for hours. Grandma came and went, and came back again, but we sat together, guarding her against the desperation of the illness. We tried to stop it from happening, but in the end, we said goodbye to her, and watched her go. Grandpa and me. Just as it had always been, but sadder, without my Mum and his daughter.

It was a difficult time, made more so by the fact that she had finally been able to stop work, and enjoy life a little, only to be hit with an illness that took her away from us, the timing seemed particularly unkind. It seemed so hugely unfair. It took time to come back from, and I will admit to falling off the rails a little. Grandpa watched and waited, and where he could, he helped. I think it was just something that I needed to do, and I no longer drink to excess. Strangely, whenever I have sat down for a beer with my Grandad, we have always drunk a toast to my Mum.

Grandma never seemed to change. She was always there, welcoming me in with a cup of tea, a slice of cake, or a biscuit.

She did this thing, from when I was little, where she stroked her hand over my head, and it was the most comforting physical gentleness. The day I came round to see them after work and she looked at me the way she had when my Mum was ill, I needed the comfort more than I ever had, but it was never going to be enough. He had seen a doctor, and, it appeared, we should be worried. We were.

He had lost a little weight, and a little of the joy that had always surrounded him, but we believed in his strength, and together we willed him, pushed him, begged him to get better.

So, today is a Wednesday, and the air is cold. I have picked up my grandpa, in the little red sports car, which I still drive, every day, and which I still love. He is in the passenger seat, and the top is down. My hair is standing on end in the cold wind. The smell of the air changes as we travel closer to the sea. My first glimpse of the water, shimmering blue in the sun is as thrilling as it was when I was a child.

"Look, Grandpa. I can see the sea." We slow, behind the traffic, and find a parking space. Slowly, we walk towards the beach. I know we are hanging it out. I want today to last. I want today to be forever. However, forever is not to be.

The beach is stony, but it gives way to sand, as we approach the water. The sun filters through the clouds, and together we make our way across the sand, and out towards the water, and the small waves that run up and down the beach. We stand together, the wind lifts our hair from our heads and our souls from the beach and up into the sky above us. I am not surprised to find that I am emotional.

Carefully and with both hands around the urn, I spill my grandpa's ashes into the breaking waves. My feet are wet, and so is my face. I could care less.

He was the man who made me strong. The man who taught me right from wrong, and who stood behind me, cheering, loving me, celebrating me, all my life. I have no clue how to move forward without him.

The sun shone down on me, when the small urn was empty. I was alone on the beach. For the first time, I truly felt I was on my own. The wind whipped across the tiny waves, picking up the salt and the water. I licked my lips, tasting the salt in the air. I remembered the kindness I had received, the love. I recalled the time spent in his care, and the joy and laughter. He had made me feel safe and strong. I had been blessed, truly and completely. I had no business feeling sorry for myself. My Mum. My Grandpa, and my Grandma had given me the tools and the strength to use them. I was the result of their hard work, and I needed, deserved, had to take everything forward, knowing that their support was behind me.

Back in the car park, I slipped the urn behind my seat, and started the engine.

"Come on, Grandpa. Let's go home." I pulled out into the traffic. "It was a good day, wasn't it?" Somewhere the gentle grey head I had loved my whole life was nodding, and I knew he was smiling. Maybe sometime soon, I would be smiling too.

31.

Our Miracle

Carrying the warm bundle, wrapped in a blanket, through the quiet early morning streets, Marie told herself, over and over that this was the best thing for the baby. She had no money, no husband, the baby would have a better life, a better family. She was doing the best thing for the baby. It was not selfishness. Except, a part of her heart screamed that the place for a baby was with her mother. Her eyes ached with the tears she had shed, but the decision was made. She stopped at the steps of St Anthony's orphanage, and reached up to ring the bell. The note she had pinned to the baby's clothes explained everything. She heard the creak of the door as it opened, and laid her baby in the arms of the woman who stood on the step, brushing her tears away, as she ran away down the street, the cries of her baby echoing off the small terraced houses on the street

When Carrie was a small child, as soon as she was old enough to understand, her adopted parents had told her about how she had come to be with them. Later, when she was naughty, as all children are, she imagined her 'real' Mummy coming to find her, so sorry for what she had done, and bringing sweeties and cuddles, not scolding or reminding her of her manners. In the back of her mind, her birth Mother remained a subject of fascination, all through her childhood and teenage years. On days when she was honest with herself, she knew her adopted parents loved her, and that she loved them right back, but there was romance and mystery in the idea of a shadowy figure in her past somewhere.

The flat was empty and quiet. The tiny pair of socks that she had kept, her only reminder of the little girl she had not been able to keep. Questions flew around her head, about the child's safety, about her own ability to make good decisions, about whether she would ever be able to forgive herself for the decision she had made.

Every year on the day that she had given birth, Marie took herself for a walk, passing by the orphanage where she had said goodbye to the child. When her life was going well, she blamed herself for her selfishness, walking away from her daughter to have things, a nice place to live, a car. When her life was going badly, she knew it was the punishment that she deserved. She almost welcomed it.

Eighteen years after the day she had given up her baby, she knocked on the door of the orphanage and asked to speak to someone about tracing her. She would be a grown up by now, and whether she was happy to see her mother or not, the waiting and self-hatred were more painful than any anger could be. If she could just know that she was alive, that she had been cared for, perhaps that would be enough.

The process was laborious. More than once, she reflected on how easily she had given up her child, and walked away, the forms she had to complete to establish contact were long and detailed, and the social workers she met were kind and helpful but she imagined that they were judging her. She was so busy judging herself, she could not blame them. Three months of waiting after the forms were submitted, before she received a letter from the social worker asking her to attend.

Wearing her best coat, she waited outside the office. Could her daughter be in the office waiting, her stomach churned on the cup of tea she had managed to swallow. The social worker opened her door and called her in, but her feet felt as though they were weighed down, or glued to the floor. It took huge effort to pull herself into the office, but it was only the social worker there. Her daughter was alive and well. Even better than that, she was prepared to meet up. A date had been set, and all she had to work out now was what to say, how to apologise, how to make up for being missing for eighteen years. She only had to wait three days, but it was going to be the three longest days of her life.

The meeting was set up for Friday morning, at eleven. She was ready, and dressed by five thirty, and pacing the floor by five forty-five. The carpet would be worn through by the time she had to leave. Finally, the hands on the clock moved around and she could leave.

The girl in the office was a stranger, but at the same time, so completely familiar. She watched eyes that looked like her own search her face, perhaps looking for something that she recognised.

"Hello. I'm Marie." She wrapped her hands around each other tightly, fighting the desire to hug her daughter.

"I'm Carrie." They both smiled widely, if warily.

"I'm so sorry. I regretted it as soon as I walked away. Thank you for meeting me. You are so beautiful, so completely lovely." Marie took deep breaths, struggling to keep the panic under control.

"Marie. I'm fine. I always wondered about you, and it is wonderful to finally meet you. My parents have been fine, I wasn't unhappy or unloved. I was just curious about you." She chewed her lower lip. "I would like to be friends, if that's OK?"

"It's better than anything I could wish for. Better than I deserve."

Marie wiped her eyes. "I brought you something." She fished out the tiny socks from her handbag, wrapped in a soft velvet bag. "I allowed myself to keep something that was yours. These have kept me company for all of these years, while I was missing you."

"Can I have a hug?" Carrie's hands fluttered at her throat.

"Oh yes, you can." Marie wrapped her arms around the magnificent woman that her daughter had become, and thanked every God in the universe for taking care of her and allowing them to find their way back to each other. "My miracle. That's what you are. Everyone gets one, you know. You are, and always have been, mine."

"Maybe we can share this one?" Carrie stood back to look at her mother, and they both swiped away the tears,

32.

Perfect Imperfection

We were almost completely incompatible. I don't mean that in the way that we lived or the jobs we did. I mean, the way we thought, the music we listened to. We disliked each other's friends. Often, we really disliked each other, but, oh, when it worked, it was stupendous.

I worked, back then, for a charity which supported people who had recently quit drugs. It was a worthwhile way to make a living, and it could be rewarding, and exhausting, and enormously frustrating.

He was a window fitter. All his friends worked in the building trade in one way or another. They called me the 'Happy Hippy,' which I thought to begin with might have been friendly banter. It was not friendly.

My friends called him 'the idiot,' I sort of thought it was meant with love. I was almost entirely incorrect.

Despite all of these issues, however, he made me laugh. Really laugh, so that I was in danger of having an accident. Sometimes, he even did it on purpose. He was blunt, to the point of rudeness, but he was honest. I trusted that he would tell me the absolute truth, even if I really had no wish to hear it.

On his side of the equation, he found my 'floucy arsedness' very annoying. Apparently, I also dithered, made excuses for plonkers, felt sorry for lame ducks, and was a complete liberal nonsense of a human. I accepted that this was his genuine belief, and that he was entitled to his opinion, but I was also entitled to disagree.

We did agree, however on a few things. He loved curries and so did I. He liked to come to my flat and tell me about his day, and how he had had argued with his customers, not one of whom, it appeared appreciated his care and effort. I told him about my day, in broad terms, without telling him any specifics, or betraying any confidences. He was interested. Sometimes, we collected a takeaway, and ate together. We enjoyed each other's company, when we were alone.

Of course, the sex was unbelievably good. I was astounded by how much difference that made. Perhaps that made me inexperienced. Previous boyfriends, if that is an acceptable term when thirty is a memory, had clearly missed a few tricks.

We spent six months of eating curries, arguing and falling into bed laughing, and it was glorious. Neither of us talked about it being a permanent arrangement, we had never spoken about living together, or anything like that, it was a happy, careless, going with the flow sort of arrangement. We talked on the phone to arrange when we would meet, or we sent texts. So, I was surprised when he left me a hand written note.

'Hey, busy til Friday. Are you free for dinner?' He wrote. I sent him a text to confirm that I was free.

He arrived with a chicken vindaloo for him and a lentil masala for me. We ate, without the jokes and the usual laughter. He was upset, or angry, or something. He said less than seven words, compared with his usual seven hundred. I imagined that he had met someone else, and steeled myself to be philosophical about it. In the end, I was not at all calm or reasoned, I drank my wine quickly and refilled my glass.

"Look, I know we're rubbish together. I don't understand half of what you talk about, and you don't like my friends." He started, pushing his lumps of chicken around.

"OK." I waited for him to tell me what he was trying to say.

"I mean. Your friends hate me." He carried on, shrugging

his shoulders. I felt that he was blaming me, for my friends' opinion.

"If you were planning to break up with me, what was the point of bringing a curry with you? Why are you being such a complete and utter arse?" My eyes stung with tears, which I fought off, and my voice was strangled by my anger.

"I wasn't planning to break up with you. I wanted to talk to you, but then as soon as I started, all the good things we normally have just went out of my head. I couldn't remember why lentils were funny even. I always laugh with you about lentils. We always giggle about bhajis and stuff. Not today, because I ruined it." He swore under his breath, and pulled his jacket on. "Call you tomorrow, Jess." There was no call the next day, though, or the day after that. I could have phoned him, but it felt wrong. I felt it was too far to reach out to him. I was hurt and angry and I maybe should have tried harder to get past that.

Life went on. I was alright, not devastated. Life was a little less shiny, I was a little sad, but there was work, and my friends, and occasionally, very much so, I met a man who would remind me that they were not him.

I had bought him a Christmas present and put it under my fake tree in my pretend happy flat. My family would be away, and my friends were having non-pretend festivities. I sat alone through the time off, wishing I could go to work, and eating the things I had bought, enough for two, even though I had no reason to expect him to be there. Nobody had told me about this, I had no idea that spending Christmas on your own was so entirely miserable. I could have phoned a friend, told them that I was sad and lonely, but I had a little bit of self-respect left, which stopped me.

I had been invited to a New Year's Eve party, which I would rather have avoided, except that I had promised my friends that I would go, so I had a bath, did my hair, and went to the loneliest thing in the world, a New Year's Eve party, when you're single, and everyone else is not. An hour at the party, spent drinking the wine I had brought with me, and I felt a little better. My friends were with me, and we danced a bit and drank more wine. Honestly, I was glad when midnight rolled around so that I could say goodbye to everyone and go home.

The Christmas tree was still up, waiting for me with its twinkling lights. I was strangely pleased to see it, as though it had waited up for me. I curled up on the couch, with a blanket and a coffee, and thought about what I would wish for in the year to come. The perfect man, the ideal relationship? Did those things even exist? His face, laughing over some silly joke drifted into my mind, and I smiled, remembering the fun we'd had, and the way he had made me feel. I had been a better version of myself with him. My imperfections had seemed less important. Perhaps that was what made the perfect relationship, the smoothing out of the bumps and blemishes in each other, because someone in your life cares.

My phone rang at a quarter to four, just as my eyes were getting too heavy to keep open. His number flashed on the screen. Panic ripped through me.

"Hello?" I answered before I had a chance to panic and hide my phone.

"Happy New Year." He whispered.

"Happy New Year too."

"Can I pop round, I want to talk to you?" I could hear his steps as he walked down the pavement. "I want to finish the conversation I started with you. My fault, and I've been paying ever since, the words are running around in my head, have been since that night. I need to say them to you, before I drive myself mad." He laughed, but the confidence was missing.

"OK, I'm home. Are you far away?" The doorbell rang.

"No. I'm here." I opened the front door. He stood on the doorstep.

"Hey. This is a bit out of the blue." I felt like I didn't know what to do next.

"Can I come in? It's freezing." I thought about it. I opened the door wider, and he walked into the flat. "Look, what I was trying to say to you, and I know I messed it up, is that we are completely wrong for each other. Your friends think I'm the thick idiot. My friends think you're a total tree hugger, but when I'm with you I feel good, better. I'm happier when I'm with you. I was trying to say that I love you. Being away from you has been bloody awful. I miss you." He stood very still, his hands firmly in the pockets of his coat.

"I missed you too." I said. I meant it. I was surprised how much. "I got you a Christmas present." His face lit up. I pointed to the tree. He ripped the paper off.

"It's the chain I liked." We had laughed about it. He had spotted the chain the in jewellers and I had told him he would look like an idiot, trying to look like a gangsta if he wore it. "I got you a present too."

He pushed his hand into his pocket and pulled out a box. Small. Black. My breath caught in my throat.

He pushed it into my hand, and I opened it, holding my breath. Inside was the biggest blingiest ring I had ever seen. We had seen it the day we had laughed about the chain. I had pointed it out as the ugliest thing in the shop.

"I told you this was ugly." I giggled.

"I figured if you would wear something you said was ugly, you might consider putting up with living with someone who is completely wrong for you, who your friends hate, and who hasn't read the right books or seen the right films, but who loves you." His eyes were deep and brown and as full of emotion as I had ever seen them.

I thought back over the last few months of missing him, and really the decision was an easy one. I slipped the ring onto my finger, and watched it glint in the flashing lights from the tree.

"I'll wear the ring, if you come with it." I told him.

He stepped towards me, and wrapped his arms around me. I felt him breathe in my scent, my hair. His hands squeezed me as close to him as he could, and I felt safe. He was my perfect imperfection, and I was his. We were perfectly imperfect together.

33.

Run Away with Me

It was perfect. I had found it on the internet, for a fraction of the price it had been in the shop. The hairdresser had been this morning, and done my hair, I was wearing the most perfect dress, my make-up was absolutely the best it had ever been. I looked tanned, toned, and probably the best I ever had. A year and a half of hard work had led to this day, and now it had arrived, and it was going like clockwork.

My Mum fluttered around me, counting down the minutes. My Dad was puffed out with pride. My best friend Julie was wearing soft pink. My nieces were dressed in tiny rose-pink dresses. I was in ivory.

My phone lay on the dressing table. I picked it up for the millionth time. Scrolling through the numbers, I found the only number I was looking for.

"Hello?" My breath hitched in my throat.

"We can't talk on the phone, can we? Isn't it unlucky, babe?" He sounded so concerned, this was what we had come to, not allowing ourselves to have a conversation with the only other person who mattered in the whole day.

"I need to talk to you. I really don't know if I can do this. Can we just go back to how it was, before we started all of this?" I remembered how lovely it had been before we stepped onto the getting married roller-coaster. We had laughed, had fun, sometimes we had just sat and watched television, without having to plan or discuss or send invitations, or make lists. "I don't feel ready. I love you, but I can't get married. I'm not a grown up."

"Don't do this. Please, don't fall apart on me. I want to be with you. Today we start a whole life together, come on Bella. We're going to have a great day, and then we'll be off on holidays. It's going to be fun." His voice wavered. "Bella, my Bella, we are standing on the edge of the rest of our life together. Come on. Let's jump together."

"Can you come round?" I sniffed. "Just for a minute. I'm sorry Ben. I just feel so shaky. Can you come round, maybe if I could see you. I would be brave enough. I don't know why this is so hard, it's what we planned."

"Your Mum would go potty!" He laughed.

"If you don't, I might not make it to the Church. Please, Ben. I don't ask you to do much for me. I'm asking this." She tried to keep the wobble out of her voice, not entirely successfully.

"For heaven's sake Bella." He huffed. "Right, OK. If your mother explodes, it's your fault."

For the next ten minutes I sat on my bed, feeling like I was nine years old, and waiting for the first day of school after long holidays, knowing that I had forgotten to do the homework. I wanted to hide in the wardrobe and come out when the whole thing was over. If I could have taken off the corset section of my dress, I would have been in jeans and a jumper, heading for my car.

"Bella?" Julie sounded worried. "Are you alright? We need to get ready to go. Your Dad says the car will be here in a few minutes."

I said nothing. I had nothing to say.

The scratchy noise of gravel hitting the window pane pulled me out of my spiral downwards. I opened the window. There in the garden, was Ben.

"Hello!" I whispered. "Thank you, Ben. I feel better just seeing you. Can we just run away? Can we do this without everyone in the world?"

"The only people who are coming to the wedding love us. Except your Grandma, who hates both of us equally. They want to wish us luck, to be part of the story of our lives. Bella, when you sit with our grandkids and show them photos from today, you can tell them that I came to your window like bloody Romeo and talked you into coming to our wedding, and making me the happiest Grandpa in the world." He held out his hands to each side.

There was silence, while I thought about what he was saying. Change. All life is about change. Our wedding day, perhaps a family. I felt as though I was standing on the edge of a cliff, he was right, I was stepping off the edge into the unknown, that was why I was frightened. Too big. Too enormous.

Then I looked down into the garden, and Ben was there. I felt so much better for having seen him. The back door flew open at that moment, and my Mother flew out, screeching like a banshee.

"Mum. Stop. I asked Ben to come over. To talk me into going to the wedding. I've decided." I closed the window so that I could hear nothing of the conversation that followed. I checked my reflection in the mirror, and straightened my veil and tiara.

My Dad was pounding up the stairs when I came out of the bedroom.

"Your Mother is about to have a heart attack. Please don't tell me that you are not going to the wedding. Ben was in the garden. Can you believe that?" He stopped at the top of the stairs, coming within a few feet of me. "Oh, my beautiful Bella. You take my breath away. You have never looked so wonderful. I am so proud." His eyes filled. He swallowed hard.

"Come on Dad. Let's go." He stepped backwards into the bathroom, so that I could get past in the huge, totally ridiculous meringue of a dress I had chosen.

The church was full, and somehow Ben, with the scolding of my mother still ringing in his ears had made it to the church before us. Without noticing the music, the flowers, even the guests, I made it to the front, and Ben.

He leaned across to me, and whispered in my ear. "Shall we run away now, or later?" I giggled.

He smiled, the smile that I loved, with all my heart, and I knew we would be alright, the change we were making would be a good one. We could run away together for the rest of our lives. We could grab the changes with both hands, so long as we were together.

34.

Space Saving

The screech of tyres and circling blue lights told me the story. I had no need to push my head out of the tree line, where I was safe. They had found us, or, more accurately, him. I stepped back, careful not to give away the advantage I had gained. I watched him being cuffed and pushed into the car.

My back rested against the side of a tree, and, as he was taken away, leaving one police car behind, I watched and waited. A message came through, I heard the crackle of the radio, and they drove off. Slowly, and carefully, I crossed the empty roadway, and slipped slowly under the fence post. Only two more fields to cover. I had lived in the area all my life. Crossing the fields in the dark was no obstacle. The heavy rucksack was wearing away the skin on my shoulders, but otherwise I was physically alright.

On the approach to the house, I stayed low, but there was no police car on the drive. No lights on at the windows. No outside lighting. It all looked as I expected. Slipping into the barn, I slid the rucksack from my shoulders, and the relief made me want to cry. The bales of hay were neatly stacked, and I moved them with the ease that comes from practice, sliding my rucksack behind one of them and pulling another over the top.

Inside I ran the bath and climbed into the hot water, my shoulders stung, and my muscles burned, but it felt good. I was out, and dressed, when the doorbell rang. The yard was brightly lit by the two cars parked there.

I counted to three, to calm my breathing and my head, before I opened the door. Two of the local constabulary's finest were waiting for me. They showed me paperwork, and I stood back to let them in. I watched them search, and they watched my reaction. The house was pulled apart, piece by piece, room by room they dismantled my home. There was nothing for them to find. Once they established that, they moved on to the barn, and the yard. I watched them check the yard, sinking their hands into the ice-cold water in the troughs. The barn was all that was left. I forced my face to stay unconcerned.

The officer came out and shook his head. They had found nothing. No word of apology, no help to clear up the mess they made. I had, of course, no room for righteous indignation.

Twenty minutes later, a knock at the window. I was expecting it, but it still made me jump. I had left the house as it was, I wanted evidence of the search.

The room was filled by the bulk of three men, each one of them big enough to snap my spine, should they choose to.

"Where is he?" They took in the ransacked house.

"Arrested." My eyes are clear and my expression level.

"Why did they take him and not you?" His face was close to mine.

"I was slower, a few steps behind. He stepped out from the tree line and they jumped on him, and I stood still." I kept my eyes on his. "They're holding him. They turned over the house, and outbuildings." I passed him the paperwork the police left.

"What will he tell them?" I shook my head and shrugged.

"He will tell them what he knows, which is that he was paid to carry the rucksack. That's it." I watched for reaction.

They waited while I retrieved my rucksack from the barn. I passed it over. He smiled. Slow and comfortable with himself.

"I'll be in touch." He dropped an envelope on the table. I watched.

We had fallen behind with the bills and the mortgage, what I made on the farm was far from being enough when Joe lost his job. The chance to make quick money had come out of nowhere, and he had taken almost no time to decide to follow my suggestion that it was for us. Now Joe was in custody.

I went to bed, having cleaned up the house, and searched for sleep. I was surprised when a noise downstairs woke me. Pulling a dressing gown around me, I crept to the top of the stairs. The relief that flooded my heart when I saw Joe in the hall was immense. I rushed down to him. His arms were wrapped around me.

"What happened Joe?" He shrugged.

"They said that they would bail me, and be in touch. They asked me what I was carrying, but I didn't know. I told them it was weights, to help me keep fit, when they stopped me, I hoped they would let me go, but they took me to the station, kept me in a little interview room. In the end they let me come home. I don't understand what this is all about. They had the rucksack, why didn't they find anything?"

"They came here and went through everything. They didn't find my rucksack though. The guys came to pick it up." We looked at each other. He had put his down by the front door.

We sat to have a cup of tea. He was more confused than anything else. The knock on the window had me up to open the door. The three men were there, to collect the second rucksack, and I confirmed that we were ready to do it again. They smiled and nodded, and they were gone.

We paid our overdue bills, and Joe went back to looking for a job. He drove me mad trying to work out what we had been carrying and why the police had not found anything. Nothing he could imagine made any sense, but who cared, when the bills were paid?

I came home from work one day to find Joe fitting a camera outside the house, it was a tiny thing, once it was up, it was impossible to see. He was becoming increasingly paranoid and thought the house was being watched, or that someone was coming there when we were out. I begged, cajoled, argued, but he was unmoved. He had to know, not knowing was driving him crazy.

Two weeks later our employers arrived, with an address to collect from, and that night, we dressed in black and trekked to the address, which was near the bay. Again, two heavy rucksacks waited for us, and this time, we made it back to the house without any interruption.

Twenty minutes after we came home, the rucksacks were collected and we were paid. Despite my pleas, that we should just take the money and not worry about it, Joe clicked onto the app to view the footage. He called me to watch with him and we both sat, our brows furrowed as we watched a van pull up to the barn, and our employers load boxes into the back of the van, before driving away. Joe jumped from his seat, as though he had won the lottery, we pulled on jackets and went out to the barn. There was nothing missing. There was a little hay on the floor which had not been there before, but nothing else looked different.

Carefully, Joe pulled a bale of hay out, then another, stacking them on the other side of the barn. I helped him. We moved the whole lot, it took hours, there was nothing there. He walked the length and breadth of the barn trying to work it out. We stacked it back where it was, and gave up.

Joe fitted another camera in the barn, and the following week we collected the rucksacks again. He could hardly wait to see what had happened.

The rucksacks were collected, and we were paid.

Joe headed to his phone. I held his arm.

"Please don't Joe. Maybe it's best we never find out. You're starting a new job next week. It doesn't matter. We don't have to do it again." He shook my hand off, gently, but firmly. He pulled up the app, and I walked away. "I don't want to see."

He sat down and clicked through the app. Another knock came on the door. I opened it, and before I could see who was there, felt a sharp pain in my face. I woke, with the feeling that my jaw was twice the size it had been earlier in the day, the front door was open, and Joe, and his phone were gone.

I went out to the barn, the cameras had been taken down, and where the one had been outside the house, just wires dangled. Joe was nowhere to be found. My face ached, I checked in the mirror, I was bruised and swollen. My head ached, my shoulder too, perhaps from where I had landed. There was a fuzzy feeling in my head, which seemed to be stuck somewhere above my eye. Moving slowly, I pulled myself onto a chair, and cradled my aching head. I was struggling to remember what happened, when the front door opened.

The police officers who searched my house stood looking at me. I watched them notice my bruising. They called for a doctor, who checked me over, nodded and told me to call if I felt dizzy or sick. The two police officers made me tea. I never drink tea.

My heart fluttered as I watched them. Police making tea for people meant they were coming with bad news. Someone had died, or been hurt. Perhaps I was still confused by the bang on my head, maybe they were hanging around because someone attacked me.

"Where's Joe?" I squinted to focus on the officer nearest to me.

"We aren't entirely sure. We came out to let you both know that no charges will be made against your husband, but he was missing, and you had been knocked out. Did your husband hit you?" I turned sharply to look at him, for which I was punished by a sharp pain across my head. I winced.

"No. I opened the door. Joe was inside, somebody hit me. That's all I remember." I watched my hands, they were steady. My wedding ring glinted on my left hand. The day Joe had put it on my finger slipped through my mind. Then the day I had finally admitted to myself that my earnings from the farm would not be enough to cover the bills. The day he had held my hand in his, rubbing his thumb over my wedding ring. I had been offered a lifeline, and had decided to take it. I had seen the way he struggled to meet my eyes. I knew he was ashamed that he was contributing nothing financially, but his attitude made it worse, he took the joy out of life, he was too knotted up with his anger and resentment over losing the job, over not being the favourite child, over the toffees his brother was given when he had none, and every other slight and petty unfairness he found in his life.

I sat at the table, the officer's eyes careful, seeking information. My eyes squinting against the light, and on one side, against the bruising. The police pushed me to remember, but I had nothing to tell them. Eventually, they had to go, and promised to send a car to check on me regularly, and made me promise that I would phone if I was concerned, or if I remembered anything.

My head hurt. The sofa looked so comfortable, and the thought that I could slip away to sleep just for a while tempted me all the way to my boots and back, but there was no time. I had something to do, and I would be late if I waited any longer.

The barn was dark, but I knew where everything was.

Hay bales are like building blocks. People see a barn with hay bales in it and they imagine it is solid. Joe was like that. He was happy to leave the heavy lifting to me, while he went to work, and later, when he stopped going to work. He had no clue what happened in the barn, and had not known for nearly two years.

When I stack my hay bales, I leave spaces, as do most farmers, to allow air to circulate, and stop damp and mould growing. It occurred to me, that if I left larger gaps, those might be useful to certain friends of mine. I could store things, on their behalf, and earn extra money for that. Trying to earn an honest living as a farmer is almost impossible. I earned a good living, none of which I could tell Joe about. I had to let us slide into debt, how could I explain the money otherwise?

When Joe lost his job, and was around more, I needed to get him out of the house to allow deliveries, and collections to be made, but he never wanted to go out, so I came up with the earning potential. We carried pointless but heavy rucksacks, giving my space renters time to collect their possessions from the barn, which is why there was nothing in the barn for Joe to find. I paid us well for the job, enough to clear the debts. I could have told him what was going on, of course I could, but he had a big mouth, he could never keep anything secret. The people who rented my spaces insisted on privacy. We would both have been gone, if their secrets had been spilled.

When he started to put up cameras, I knew it was the end. No matter how much I argued with him, he insisted. It was out of my hands. There was nothing I could do to save him. These were powerful and ruthless people, and he was interfering with their business. I took a smack in the face. Joe was gone, and he would not be coming back. My clients would continue to rent the space in my barn, and I would not have to listen to the list of things that had gone wrong for Joe, and how the world was not fair. I would miss him.

In the barn, in the dark, I moved the bales. I heard the sound of an engine outside and cracked the door to take a look. The van was backing into the barn, and in less than ten minutes the loading was complete.

I took my bruised face inside, and tucked a blanket around myself on the sofa. Sleep came easily.

35.

The Garden Gate

Living in this wonderful house has been such a treat, the first year has been hard work, fixing up everything, and trying to get control of the garden. The views across the fields make working in the garden a pleasure, and frequent breaks, spent leaning on my shovel have let my muscles rest between bouts of digging.

The flowers have come and gone, and the veggies I planted have been eaten, some by us, and some by the wildlife, who wander through. The time has come to dig over the patch, and, I will need to dig deeper this time, to move some large bushes from other places around the garden, and then dig again, in the new veggie patch which I have picked out, and fenced, in the vain hope that we might keep a little more of the crop for ourselves.

The sun was shining, and it was still warm, although it was the end of October, and I was looking forward to a morning spent digging and taking tea breaks.

The plants were dried up and shrivelled, they put up no objection to being pulled out, and loaded into my wheelbarrow. Then the digging began, as deep as two shovel lengths, lifting and turning, then moving forward to the next line. My back ached and my boots sunk in the wet soil, but it was the perfect place for me to be, and I knew that my hand work would be rewarded in the spring, when the bushes I would plant would burst into leaf, and then flowers, and I would know that I had made the right decision about this part of the garden.

After two hours of alternating between digging and taking a break I stopped for a cup of tea, sipping the hot liquid, sitting on the wooden edging. I was nearly half way along the border, and I had set myself the goal of reaching the half way mark before I took another break, so it was back into the mud, which caked around my boots, and stuck to my shovel, and continuing in the same way as before. Except that when I pushed my shovel into the ground, it jarred my shoulder, hitting something hard. I presumed that I would find another lump of rock, to join the growing pile, but instead, I found the corner of a red brick.

Shrugging my sore shoulder, and wondering why someone would leave a brick busied in the garden, I heard a noise on the lane, above the bank, about level with my shoulder.

"Hello. You look busy." I had spoken to the man before, and had always called him the Colonel in my head, he had a military way of holding himself, despite his age, and a cut glass accent which I found endearing.

"I'm digging up the veggie patch. I was going to put it over the other side, and have flowers and bushes here. What do you think?" I rested my sore shoulder, by leaning against the shovel.

"Sounds a good idea. I shall look forward to seeing it grow on my walk each morning. Don't overdo it with the digging." He waved and marched off down the lane.

Living in a small village is lovely, but you really cannot sneeze without people knowing and wanting to know why. I had nicknames in my head for most of the neighbours. Mrs Vague, The Colonel, Mrs Very Cross and Mr On the Run. They were lovely people, except for Mrs Very Cross. I was convinced that Mr On the Run had embezzled some money or something and was hiding out. They probably had a funny name for me too.

I shovelled again, and found the rest of the brick, then again, and again. I moved further across the border and dug down again, and again. Perhaps there was a path under the soil. It was about six inches down, but it might be pretty. I changed my plans and started excavating the path. An hour later, and I had three rows of bricks, laid across the border, another hour gave me three more. It was a path. It ran across the border to the bank. Perhaps there had been steps, and a gate there once, I wondered. Why would the previous owners have moved the entrance, looking at it now, it made more sense to have the gate there. It was in line with the house.

"Hello. My goodness you've been digging a lot." Mrs Vague was standing on the lane above me.

"Hello. Yes, I have found a path, I think. I wonder if there used to be a gate onto the lane here?" I looked up, and she looked away, distracted.

"Not that I remember, dear." She waved and wandered on, further up the lane, leaving me to my digging.

Clearing the mud left me a path and five steps, almost to the level of the lane. Where the hedge now blocked what had been an entrance. Deciding that I had earned my lunch, I put the tools away and took myself back to the house. I was curious though, about the steps, and the pathway, and went in search of the deeds. Finding the old plans, I traced my finger along the boundary line, and found a break in the line, almost where I had been digging. That had to be what it was, an old pathway and gate. Perhaps it was left over from before everyone had a car and needed to park on a driveway.

I swept away the rest of the mud on the bricks, and wondered about the possibility of opening up the gateway again. It would be easier to get to the house from there. I was tired though, and in any case, the first fat cold drops of rain that had been threatening for the last half hour had fallen. I pushed the tools back into the shed and went inside for a hot bath.

It rained over-night and, in the morning, I found that the mud around the pathway had washed away, and the bricks were wobbling. I was a little worried, they seemed quite unstable. It seemed sensible to take the bricks out, it was unlikely that I would use the path, and it might collapse. Better to take it out.

I lifted the first row of bricks easily enough, and began to work my way further back, towards the steps. The mud was thick and wet from the rain, and it lay heavy on my shovel. Lifting the bricks was hard work, and I was glad for each visit from each of my neighbours and the chance they gave me to stop for a break. After the first three rows, I found the going was getting harder, lifting each one with a squelch noise, pulling against the suction of the wet mud. It was difficult, but I was making progress. The dark clouds overhead, however, had different plans, and I was forced back inside while the sky threw wind and rain at the garden and the house.

The next day I pulled my boots on and zipped up my coat. The pathway was waiting for me, the rain had washed away the mud, and there were thick roots running out under the path. I pulled at one, sighing, this was turning into a bigger job than I had thought.

The root came free, with a little wiggling, and I pulled. It was caught, I pulled a little harder, and it came loose. There was a whole web of them. I smiled, they looked like a hand, bones. I took a breath, they were hard, cold in my hand. I felt the weight. These were not roots.

I felt the sting of the slap on the side of my head, but not the next time the shovel hit me. I was unconscious, and soon, I was further, deeper, colder. My neighbours had been hiding something. Now they had more hiding to do.

36.

The war that came to a party

I was an arrogant child. Everyone agreed. Too cool for school. Too convinced of my own opinion. I decided, after school finally gave up on trying to keep me in, that I would spend a year in another country. My budget was almost zero, so I had to find a way to work while I was away. My parents threw up their hands in horror, at the thought of my living so far from home, in another country, a completely different culture, where women generally were viewed so differently. Beirut was then, though, a playground for the rich and famous, and I thought it would be glamorous. I had pestered my grandparents, my aunts and uncles, and anyone who would listen, and scraped together the money for the flight. The plane landed, and I was taken to the family home.

The house was surrounded by a high wall, and protected by strong gates. The children were nice, we played a lot, I enjoyed them, I made them laugh and we became friends. The cleaning and the laundry was, it turned out, not so glamorous as I had imagined. I learned to make the thick dark coffee that my employer liked. They were indeed the rich and powerful people I had imagined, but that made no difference to me. Washing the dirty clothes which belong to the golden people is the same as doing laundry in Croydon.

"We shall have to educate you, little Molly." My employer would say, when I would make mistakes. His eyes, dark and hooded, dancing with humour, hinted at teaching me about more than coffee.

My employers, a beautiful olive-skinned man, and his sharp featured, angry wife, entertained often. Other beautiful people would arrive, eat, drink, laugh too loud and leave. I was ordered to stay out of the way at all times.

The night of the big party, I was instructed to keep the children out of the way. I had made them tired, running all day so that they would sleep, but they were too wired to rest. The caterers arrived, as well as the waiting staff, young men who lounged about beneath the trees and watched the children running.

We sat, me, and the three little faces which had become so dear to me, watching the cars as long as buses pull into the driveway, lit by a thousand tiny lights. We ate the tiny pastries I had brought from the kitchen, and imagined what it would be like to be in the huge cars, dressed in such beautiful clothes. Once they had all arrived, the children agreed there was nothing left to see, and I tried to convince them to go to bed. They refused, high on the excitement of the night, and the sugar from the pastries.

On condition that they were very quiet, I let them come with me to the laundry room, where I had work to do. They liked the little room, where the big machines hummed all day to clean the clothes, and where I burned myself on the iron trying to press them. They helped to sort the washing, and we loaded the machine. Soon the warmth of the room, and the rhythmic sounds of the machine lulled them to sleep on the piles of clean sheets waiting to be pressed, safe inside the tent I had made for them out of the blankets I had washed the day before that hung on rails to air.

The first I that I knew of something being amiss, was a loud bang, followed by another. The children stirred in their sleep, but slept on. I opened the door a crack, and heard screaming, and another loud bang, a man shouted something I did not understand, and a woman screamed. I pushed the door closed as quietly as I could, and switched off the iron.

Slipping behind the blankets with the children, who were sitting up now, bleary from sleep, I whispered to them that they must stay very still and quiet. Their dark eyes, huge saucers in the half light, filled with fear. I lay down with them, and covered us over with the sheets. Holding them close to me, we stayed where we were. The sounds drifted through to us on the night air. Screams and muffled shouts made us hold each other tighter.

When I heard the slap of shoes on the tiled floor in the hallway, I thought my heart would stop. I squeezed my arms tighter, hoping that the children understood to be still. The door opened slowly, and I held my breath, hoping that whoever was there would not hear out hearts beating out of our chests. In the semi-darkness I could see my fear reflected in the children's dark eyes.

The door closed again, and I heard doors to the other rooms further down the hall open and close. Then nothing. No sound. No more bangs or screams. We stayed where we were. My arm, crushed by three little heads was numb, and painful, but I kept it there, unwilling to risk being found out by a small movement.

When the sun filtered through the window, the children were asleep, and I was able, very slowly to move my arm out. The oldest opened his eyes, and looked at me. I whispered to him to stay where he was, and I crawled out to look.

The main living room was strewn with bodies, my beautiful people had been butchered, their lifeless eyes stared at the empty spaces where artwork had hung. I used the telephone in the kitchen to call for help, which came, and I took the children out of the back door so that they did not have to see their parents look like that. They went to live with their grandparents, and I was no longer needed, their hugs and kisses goodbye strained my resolve to be strong for them, and their silent acceptance of their grandmother's sharp instructions broke my heart.

They said it was political, but I saw the bodies, and the jewellery that was no longer there. The artwork taken from the walls. Unless political is some kind of covert, undercover way of saying stealing, they were wrong. The young men who should have been serving canapes and champagne, served up bullets and death. I was told later that this was a war, but it seemed nothing like that to me. It was terrifying and dreadful, and it stole the beautiful people from their children.

I came home to the rain and the greyness, where nobody was beautiful or glamorous, but everyone was alive. Sometimes, even now, I wake feeling the weight of those three little heads on my arm, and the fear of discovery in my heart.

My life moved on, I met a man and had babies of my own to look after, and now, they are grown up, and moved out to get on with their own lives and loves, just as everyone should. Every time I walked back into the house in the evening, and put dinner on the table and watched my children eat, I thanked whatever goodness there was in the universe, that my children had grown up with both parents alive and interested in their welfare and loving them with everything that we had to give. Every night, I put them to bed, and said a silent thank-you that they were safe.

I get letters from the three little children, and I write to them. They are grown up now, and they have children of their own, and are very important, but they remember the day when a young girl employed to improve their English, kept them safe wrapped in laundry, while we listened to the gun shots, that took their parents and the important friends, condemning them to a strict religious upbringing with their grandparents and stealing them away from the life they had known.

The sounds and the sights of that night have stayed with me, for all of my life. The war that was started against the beautiful, rich, privileged people at the party seemed to me to be jealousy. I may not fully understand the politics or the religious arguments, but it seemed to me that fighting a war against partygoers armed with jewellery and perfume was wrong, and anything that they gained from it could only poison their lives, not further their dreams.

The worst picture that stays in my head was the children's

bedroom, after it was all over and I went to pack their clothes. The gunmen must have thought a pillow under the covers was one of the children, and shot a bullet through the sheet. How could a child be your enemy? I have no understanding of what happened that night, or so many other nights when violence has been unleashed against those who cannot protect themselves. Beirut is now recovering from the years of war which left the buildings speckled with bullet holes and the generation who lived through it, as scarred and damaged as their city. I was invited to visit, by one of the children I loved, but I think perhaps my days of travelling to that part of the world are over.

37.

The Visitor

The town I grew up in was small, the sort of place where everyone knew everything about you, and your family. My Mum worked hard, with two jobs, and whenever she had ten minutes and could keep her eyes open, she read the cards, mostly for girls who wanted to find love, or whatever. I used to watch them turn up, whispering to each other, giggling. They said she was a Witch, but, when I asked her, she said that was just them being silly and wanting to frighten each other.

My Dad was the local no hoper. She had met him when she was young, and within a year, they were married, and I was on the way. He had never, that I remembered, had a proper job. He usually owed money to people, using up his government money paying back last week's loans, before taking out a new one. He was the worst kind of role model, he drank and smoked, and slept until noon most days, but I loved him. My Mum let him stay in the house, bus she had rules. He stayed in the room they had built in the garden, and he stayed away from her.

I came home from my job helping an old lady down the street with her garden, and there was shouting. It happened sometimes. She stormed back into the house, leaving the back door to slam itself behind her.

I put the money I had earned gardening on the table and washed my hands in the sink. The house was quiet, except I could hear noises from upstairs. Drying my hands on the back of my jeans, I followed the sounds, and found my Mum folding and putting things away in her bedroom. The normally tidy space was strewn with clothes and underwear.

"What happened?" I sat down on the bed next to her.

"He was looking for my savings. Hah, where would I get savings from?" I held her hand.

"What are we going to do?"

"I'm just not having it anymore. I've supported and defended that man for the last time. Sorry Janey, he's crossed the line."

I had no idea what that meant. I was fairly sure it was bad. The doorbell rang, and she straightened her top and checked her hair in the mirror. Downstairs three girls waited to be told that they were going to meet someone special, and that he would love them forever.

Later, when I got hungry, I went downstairs, and there was my Mum, sitting at the table with the cards laid out in front of her. She was looking at something far away, and I slipped out the back door to go and meet a friend who lived around the corner.

Ruth and me, we had been friends for ever. We used to sit and dream about how we would leave town, get to a big city and start a real life. Most evenings in the summer, we walked up to the main road, and talked all the way there, and all the way back.

We were walking along the pavement when we heard his motorbike, the roar of the big engine, as he screamed through the town. We turned, mouths open, and watched him pull up outside my house.

He was the tallest man I had ever seen, and thin too. The leather of his jacket was scuffed and scratched, and his hair was long and black. We were breathless, and silent. He turned and looked at us, standing on the side of the road.

"Stay there." He pointed at us. We nodded. He pulled out two huge knives, and twisted them through wide arcs, so that they flashed in the evening sun.

We followed the man, of course we did. He walked past my

house and straight to the room in the garden, where he kicked the door open. Twice, amid the screams and thuds my dad tried to leave, but the man pulled him back in. Then there was silence. It felt like forever. Ruth and me sat on the grass, and waited, and waited.

It was fully dark, and still we sat. The strange thing was that in our town, if anything happened, people came to see, but not that night. It was late. The moon was up and still we sat.

When the man came out, he walked past the house.

"Go to bed Janey, Ruth." He growled. We took one look at each other and we ran for our beds. I watched him climb on his bike first though.

The next morning, I woke up to the sound of power tools. Outside my dad was fixing the gate and weeding the flower beds.

"Morning Janey. Can't stop, I have to get ready for an interview for a job." He was whistling, actually whistling.

My Mum was inside putting her cards away, carefully where they always went, in the cupboard on the left.

"What happened?" I watched her face, but she had nothing but smiles and shrugs.

People said later that she had summoned a demon, that it was witchcraft or magic, nobody had ever seen such a dramatic change in a man. No more gambling or drinking. Full time employment. He was brand new. People asked me what I knew, but I could only shrug my shoulders and be glad.

Nobody knew who he was, or why he was in town that evening, but I can tell you, life was different from then on.

38.

Dance with me

The nursing home smelled of industrial cleaning fluid, and wee. The old girls were sitting in the lounge. The television was on, but most of them were snoozing. This was my favourite time of the day, lunch was out of the way, and everyone was comfortable. The sunshine slanted its way in through the wide windows, making shapes on the carpet, and the quiet snores of the residents made the room feel comfortable, and happy. I made a cup of tea for myself, and spotted that Maggie was awake. I took her a cup over.

"Here you go, lovely." Her face crinkled into a smile, her watery blue eyes twinkling at me. The cup rattled in the saucer, but she kept it upright. She took a sip, and nodded.

"Thanks Natalie. That's very nice." She sipped again. "Look at all of them, sleeping away the days." She shook her head. "I have better things to do." She patted my hand.

"Got a hot date?" I waggled my eyebrows at her.

"There was a time, back when I was your age, that I had loads of dates." She put the cup down on the table. "Do you want to come with me?" She held out her hand. I looked at her palm, the lines ran deep across it. I laid my hand gently in hers. It would not be the first time I had danced an old lady around the lounge.

"I wouldn't miss it for the world." I gripped her hand. The ceiling fans turned, the lights flashed and flickered, the room spun. I felt a little bit sick, and looked at Maggie's calm happy face.

We were in a room, there was a bed with dresses covering it. The woman holding my hand was my age, she pulled a dress off the bed, and slipped it over her head, so that it slipped over the petticoat she was wearing.

"Choose one Natalie." I looked at her, unsure what to do. "Come on, we only have an hour or so." Shrugging my worries away, I picked up a soft red dress, with tiny flowers all over it. I peeled off my uniform and wiggled my way into the dress. "Shoes." She demanded. I slipped my feet out of the sensible shoes, and into the heels she pushed my way. "Right. Lipstick. A bit of rouge." I followed instructions. "Turn around." She ran a pencil up the back of my legs. "Time to go."

We pulled on coats, and linked arms down the road. The night was dark, and the street lights were out. Her eyes were the same, the wrinkles were gone. She steered me up some steps, and into a dance hall. All around the room, couples danced. A band filled the stage, and the music was familiar, it sounded like a thousand black and white movies. The men were all in uniform, smart, tinged with desperation. I turned to her.

"What's going on Maggie?" She twinkled her smile at me.

"I learned how to do this from my Mum. This is where I slip off to when I get the chance. This is my best time, before I got busy with a house, and kids, and all that nonsense. This is when I had fun." A man in a smart uniform came across the room towards us.

"Good evening Maggie, who is your friend?" His accent sounded American.

"Hello, how are you? This is Natalie." She gestured to me like a magician's assistant.

"Good evening Natalie. I wondered if you might like to dance." He smiled, like he was auditioning for a toothpaste commercial. He was lovely looking, and I had been going through a bit of a dry patch since I split up with Dave. What the hell, I might not have a clue how to do this kind of dancing, but I was going to have a go.

"I'd love to, but I warn you, I'm not a very good dancer." His hand was in front of me, so I dropped mine into his. He led me out onto the floor, and squeezed me against him, his hand firm in the middle of my back, while we swayed around the room.

"Natalie. That's a lovely name. I'm Joe. You're a better dancer than you think." His hand squeezed mine. The band took a break, and he held my hand all the way back to where Maggie had been sitting. "May I get you a drink?" I nodded, and he disappeared, returning with a glass of something that smelled pretty grim. I smiled up at him. This was the most romantic thing that had ever happened to me. Dave had never danced with me, not once had he held me the way Joe had. Or rushed off to get me a drink. I sipped from the glass and caught him looking at me. This was wonderful, fabulous, not the drink, that was disgusting. The whole thing. The dancing, the handsome man in front of me, the band and the twinkling lights. A fantasy. Maggie twirled past me with a man in a dark uniform, wrapped in his arms and smiling like she had lost the plot.

The howling noise took me by surprise. Everything stopped. Everyone stopped. Maggie was next to me, and we were pushed along with the crowd through the doors we arrived through and up the street. She held my hand. Everyone was going down into the underground. The sirens wailed and we stepped carefully down into the darkness. Wartime London was a dark and scary place, but her attitude and his warm hand made it feel a little safer.

Sitting down in the tunnels, while everything above us was pounded and set alight, with Maggie on my left and Joe on my right, I tried to focus my brain, but it was stuck. I was so scared. This was so real. Each thump and bang over our heads made me clutch both of them closer. My eyes tight shut, against the fear and possibility we could be stuck here.

Somewhere further down the platform someone started singing. I had sung the songs with the old ladies over and over, but it had never felt like this. Maggie squeezed my hand and waved it backwards and forwards with the song. We sang together, as we had so many times. Joe joined in and, although we ducked and flinched with every bang and thump, it felt better like we were in it together. When the all clear sounded, we followed the crowd up the stairs. We walked back to Maggie's place, and Joe kissed me. It was gentle and sweet and soft, and kind. His hands wrapped around my waist, and pulled me close to him, but that was it, he didn't grab a fumble, didn't squeeze my arse. It was rather wonderful. He walked away and I watched him go. A part of me wanted to go with him.

Maggie opened the door, and we slipped inside. The bedroom was as we left it, and we pulled our old clothes back on. She grabbed my hand and looked into my eyes. I held her stare, and we were back in the lounge. I sat back into the chair, feeling light headed.

"Shit." I whispered. "What happened, Maggie?" She took a deep breath.

"Are there any biscuits over there in the cupboard." I nodded. "Any chance of a fresh cup of tea? I'll show you how it's done." I made her the tea and brought her biscuits.

Of course, everyone started to wake up then, and I had to make tea for them, and bring more custard creams. Then it was time for a sandwich and a bowl of soup. I kept trying to sit down and chat to Maggie, but every time I got close, something got in between us. Then it was bedtime, and another carer took her off to bed.

Later, I slipped into her room, she was still awake, but drifting. I sat down on the edge of the bed, and held her hand.

"Thank you, Maggie, for taking me with you, I had the best fun." I felt her fingers wrapping around mine in the dark.

"I'll show you how to do it tomorrow. Then you can go back and see Joe." She chortled quietly. I left her to sleep, and an hour later, I was on my way home, seeing the streets in a different way. The rain had washed the pavements clean, and for the first time in my life I was truly grateful, and understood how lucky I was not to live in a time when a siren might sound to warn you that everything you love, and everyone you ever cared about could die in the next ten minutes.

In the morning, I was on an early shift, almost bouncing in through the door. The manager met me in the dining room.

"Natalie, can I have a word?" She was all sharp edges and good tailoring. I raised my eyebrows. "I know you have been working closely with Maggie Reid. I wanted to tell you before you went in. Maggie passed away last night, peacefully, in her sleep." I sat down fast. I had been dancing with her yesterday. She had been so full of life. We had laughed and joked, she had been so young and full of life. "Make yourself a cup of tea and take half an hour to get yourself together." She patted my arm in a distant sort of way, that made me dislike her.

I did as I had been told, made my tea, and took some biscuits out of the tin. Maggie had been the nicest old lady, and the most fun as a young girl out on the town.

The lounge was quiet, the grey grape vine was working overtime, and everyone had heard that Maggie had gone.

I took the bags from the linen cupboard, and went in to Maggie's room to strip the bed, and tidy up. I had never heard her talk about a family. But it had surprised me before, when someone died how a family could pop up out of nowhere. The bed stripped, a fresh cover smoothed over, and the room tidied, I pulled a yellow rose from the vase on the window sill, and placed it on her pillow.

"That's sweet." I felt her hand in mine. "You're a good girl. Always were the best one here. Take a look on the book shelf. I reached up, and ran my fingers along the spines. Poetry, short stories, a bible, a romance set in wartime London. "That one." I pulled it out, and turned around. She was dressed for the dance hall. "Keep the book, darling Natalie." She whispered. I pushed it into my pocket, wondering if I had imagined the whole thing. The manager let me go home early, and I was glad to go.

I sat on my bed and pulled the book out of my pocket. It was a romance, a young nurse and a Canadian airman, named Joe. I read it, smiling, until I found the scrap of fabric she had used as a bookmark. Red, with tiny flowers on it. I held it in my hand, and my heart beat a little faster. My room stalled, and I was back, in my red dress and my heels, with Maggie next to me, and we were off to a dance. I stopped walking, and wrapped my arms around her.

"I missed you." I told her.

"No. I nearly missed you." She smiled that twinkly blue eyes smile at me, and I knew we would be going dancing.

39.

Meet Me

The evening sun made eerie shapes in the forested landscape, the trees throwing shadows across her path. When she had agreed to meet him in Devils Wood, she had thought it was exciting, breaking the rules set by every family in the village for their children. Everyone had grown up hearing the stories, the warnings, the finger-wagging, head shaking dire cautionary tales that had kept the woods out of bounds all her life. It was the first time she had been in the woods more than three feet. Games of dare and the pushing and shoving, screaming terror of her younger years were over. This was a dare beyond anything she had done before.

He had whispered to her, his breath hot against her ear, that if she was brave enough, she would meet him, she would break the rules. She knew that he meant her to break more than the rule not to go into the woods.

Stepping carefully over the tree roots which threatened to trip her feet, she searched in the half light for the big oak tree he had talked about. A screech to her left made her jump, then steady herself with a hand against the tree. Her breathing was a little deeper than it should be, her heartbeat a little faster. The shade of the trees cooled the air around her. The light dappled through the leaves, and fading fast, the shade took more of the space.

She stepped forward, telling herself to be brave. In her mind she pictured his face, when he had stood next to her, his fingers grazing hers, his words whispered into her ear, his stolen kisses when nobody was looking. Ahead of her, looking through the trees, she could see a huge oak. She hoped there was only one. The darkness gathered around her, like a cloak on a cold day. Each step took her closer to the tree, yet she seemed to get no nearer. She walked as fast as she dared, careful to lift her feet high over the tree roots. Slowly she felt she was getting closer.

It was fully dark by the time she reached the tree. The rough bark hard against her fingers. She took a breath, and leaned back against the trunk, closing her eyes and hoping that she would not have to wait too long.

"Peter. Peter, are you here?" She called softly. There was no reply. What if his parents had caught him, and stopped him from coming to meet her? Perhaps he would not come, and she would wait here the whole night, alone in the darkness. She refused to be dissuaded by the fear that knotted itself around her stomach, and squeezed. She would, one day, tell her children, she imagined, how she had crept from her mother's house to meet their Father in the woods. She had no doubt that Peter was the one. The one she would spend her life with, and raise a family.

A creak in the tree's branches pulled her mind back to the present. The darkness meant that she could not see up into the branches above her.

"Peter? Are you there?" A thud behind her made her spin to scan through the dark. She could see nothing. She felt her way forward, her hands in front of her, falling over a root, and crawling forwards. Until her fingers felt something among the leaves. She felt it with her fingers, identifying it as a shoe, much larger than she would have worn. Her eyebrows scrunched together, as she tried to imagine why a shoe would fall from a tree. She looked up, into the dark branches, but she could see nothing.

A puzzle. Who would leave a shoe in the woods? The wind was starting to pick up, and the clouds high above her moved, letting the moon slip out, to shine some light down between the branches. She looked up, and there, above her, was Peter. His scarf, which she had so admired, was wrapped tightly around his neck, and his eyes bulged, as his body slowly swayed in the breeze, with one shoe still on his lifeless foot.

Perhaps, people said later, he had reached the tree early and decided to climb the tree to surprise her, his scarf catching on a branch, and hanging him when he slipped. Or perhaps the stories had been true about the cursed woods and the dangers they held. Either way, she would never step foot between the trees again, or take so lightly the warnings of her family and friends.

40.

Balance

After a long day at work, when nothing seemed to go the right way, and eating dinner alone, again, she watched the street through her window, he was missing again. He was late, not answering his phone, fallen off the planet, again.

She poured a cup of tea, and added milk. It was starting to rain. It suited her mood. There was nothing she wanted to watch on tv, and everything on her computer irritated her. Even her cup of tea, her usual go to comforter was not hitting the spot. Hitting redial on her phone took her to his voicemail again.

Was it possible that he was seeing someone else? A tear slipped down her cheek. The chance that he was betraying her trust, made a bubble of hurt fill her chest. Had she become boring? Perhaps she worked too many hours, was too driven, too tired when she came home.

Slipping off her shoes in the bedroom she put them into the wardrobe that she had bought and paid for, pulled out some comfortable joggers and a t-shirt, pulling off the skirt and blouse she had worn to work. She wiped the make-up from her face, and let her hair loose from its workday bun. The house was warm. She pulled a face, she had checked her bank statement that morning, the payment for the electricity had been taken. Was that why he was staying away? Did she go on about how much she paid for too much? Was she bitter about it? Was he?

She had earned more than he did when they met, but only just. It had not mattered at all, they had fallen in love, rolling across the beach and into the sea, then back, covered in sand and laughing through the shower and into bed. It had been the best thing that ever happened to her, and she had thought that he felt the same way. That had been five years ago. They rarely had time to go to the beach these days, her work took up more and more of her time, she left the house early, dressed in suits and heels, and came home tired. Climbing the corporate ladder had taken huge effort but it had been worth it, for both of them. She chewed her lower lip, was this her fault, perhaps she had concentrated on work too much, and not given him enough attention. Had he felt side-lined?

The self-blame irritated her. If he couldn't see that she was working for both of them, then that was just him being stupid. He could get over it, and stop being a child.

Pouring the cold tea down the sink, she opened the fridge, and poured herself a glass of wine, watching the liquid swirl and fill the bowl of the glass. She had learned to accept that not everyone accepted her hard work or her commitment to her career. Over the years she had been forced to deal with jealousy, anger, and sometimes even aggression. She had sometimes taken time alone in the ladies, to cry a few tears, and then she had wiped her face, straightened her skirt and taken their criticism on the chin. No tantrums or loss of her calm professionalism.

She turned on the tv, and let the sound and pictures wash over her. This was different, it was not a clash over a promotion, or a challenge to her authority. This was the man that she loved. She did still love him. A tear slipped from her eye. She phoned him again. Voicemail.

The sound of his key in the door had her on her feet. Telling herself to stay calm, to hear him out. Her nails digging into the soft skin on the palms of her hands. Every last piece of her control called into action.

"Hey. I've been trying to reach you. I was worried." His t-shirt was splattered with paint.

"Yeah? I was a bit busy. Did you eat?" He walked into the kitchen and put together a sandwich. He knew she had eaten. She was hungry when she came home from work.

"What have you been doing?" Trying hard to keep the edge out of her voice.

"Do you want to know?" He took a bit of the sandwich. Chewing hard.

"Yes. I really do." She waited.

"I've been doing a bit of work." He held his t-shirt out to show her. "Painting."

"It's late for painting." She swallowed the rest of what she wanted to say.

"No, not really. Would you like to see the job?" He slipped the last of the sandwich into his mouth.

"Yes. I'd like that." She pulled on a coat and trainers.

"Come on then." There was some urgency in his voice, and she followed him down the stairs, and into his car.

He drove away from the house, and through the darkness, through the roads she knew so well. The car park was fairly empty, and he slotted his car carefully into a space.

"You're doing a painting job here?" She was surprised, it seemed unlikely.

"Come on." He jumped out of the car, and she followed him. The tarmac of the carpark giving way to the shingle and then the sand of the beach.

Ten feet ahead of her, he stopped, holding his arms out to his sides, like a magician showing his best trick. She slowed as she came nearer to him. A smile covering her face. This was something that they had talked about all those years ago.

A beach hut, standing out from the others, painted pale blue, with tiny lights hung from the roof in sweeping loops. The windows were hung with pretty curtains, and inside, the walls were the same pale blue, and hung with tiny lights. There was a bed, white bedding, with big squashy cushions and a bottle of cold wine, sitting in an ice bucket, condensation dripping down the glass. It was beautiful, it snatched her breath away.

"It's what we talked about, it's our dream." She turned to him. "It's perfect. Wonderful." The tears that had threatened to fall earlier, when she had imagined him with someone else, fell now, when she could see that he had been with her all the time.

He covered the space between them, and pulled her into his arms. His lips gently gazing hers.

"I've been too busy with work. I haven't made the time. I'm sorry." She returned the kiss.

"I know you're just working for us. I've been a bit of a spoilt child. I'm sorry too."

Tumbling, rolling like they had when love was new, hot and heavy in their own very special beach space, the sound of the waves surrounding them.

Later, when they sat drinking the wine that he had chilled, in the space that he had made, and the time that she had taken. She reflected, that life might be a struggle sometimes, with sacrifices and hard work needed to reach the goals they had set themselves, but they would keep this space as theirs. A place where they could escape the pressures and find each other. They would find a way to balance.

41.

Flying High

"Tower, this if foxtrot tango two nine, requesting clearance for take-off."

"Foxtrot tango alpha two nine, please taxi to the runway, you are cleared for take-off." The voice was one she knew well.

"Thank you tower. Send my love to Carrie. See you soon." She pushed the throttle forward and taxied to the end of the runway, flipping through the last checks on the instruments which had become second nature to her over the last few years.

"Fly safe Maria." The radio crackled.

The last turn onto the runway made, she lined up the small plane in the centre, and took a breath. This was the part she loved. Throttle back, and she was speeding towards the end of the small airfield, pulling back on the yoke, she lifted the plane away from the earth and her breathing slowed. This was where she wanted to be, where she lived. Pilots would tell each other that flying was boring, no different to driving a lorry or a bus, but she knew they were lying. Freeing herself from the earth was the best way, the only way, to live.

It was, however, expensive. Each trip took fuel, then there was insurance, storage, and the cost of maintenance. She thought about the costs while she lifted up to a thousand feet, and steadied out. Her flight plan, carefully completed and logged, was a lie. She was not heading to the south coast, or at least she would not be stopping there.

The flight was uneventful, and she touched down in a small

airfield in Northern France in the early afternoon. Her contact greeted her, as he always did, with a kiss, a package to deliver, and a bag of cash for her. Happy days.

She ate a little lunch, while the plane was refuelled, and with a wave and smile, she was ready to fly again. The field was wide and flat, perfect. She had no need to call the tower as there was none. She gave the plane enough throttle, and pulled back to lift the little plane over the trees. She set her instruments to take her home, and flew low over the sea and back to England. The flight was the same one she made two or sometimes three times a month. She had never asked what was in the package, nor did she want to know. She knew exactly what was in her payment. Same as every other time.

Calling ahead to the airfield at Elstree, to ask for permission to land, she was told to circle as the runway was in use. She circled wide around the field, and over her house, sliding the window open and dropping the package and her payment onto the roof of the garage. She completed the circuit and landed neatly, pulling up outside the hangar, parallel to three other small planes. The mechanic was waiting to check the plane over, and she smiled when she saw it was an old friend.

"Hey Phil. How are you?" She swung down from the door.

"Maria. Good to see you." She waved and made her way to the car park. The day was clear blue skies all the way, so she pushed the button to open the soft top. Her hair was short, and blew back from her face as she drove the short distance to her house.

The remote opened the garage door and she was in, and the door was closing behind her before she switched off the engine. In the garage, she leaned the ladder against the wall, and popped the skylight open. The two packages were where I left them.

The cash went straight into the safe. The other package went into the bottom of a grocery bag, with sugar, flour and a loaf of bread on top.

Groceries locked into the boot of the car, she drove to the shopping centre. The car park was full, but she found a space around the back, and spotted her contact in a black truck. She waved. He smiled and jumped out and crossed to meet her. They met half way, and he took the bag from her. That was it. All done.

Last stop, for her other big expense. The door swung easily when she pushed it. She punched in the code to open the inner lobby and slid through, past the day room and the lingering scent of over-cooked cabbage. Her mother sat on the bed. "Hello Mum. How was your day today?" The wave of confusion which crossed the face she loved hurt in places she could not protect. She dredged a smile up from somewhere else, and pushed it onto her face. "Look, I bought you chocolate." A wary hand reached across the distance and took the sweets. It had become as real a currency as her ability to fly, or the cash that she was paid for it.

42.

Whores and Assassins

The cabin in the mountains was almost hidden by the trees, close to the treeline, and covered in snow. Its remoteness was part of the appeal, and had been for many years. The outside was rustic in appearance, and bore no resemblance to the sumptuous interior. For decades, perhaps longer, this had been the place where the top echelons of society had come to relax and be entertained. Now that the country was being run by the military invaders, they had adopted the same habits as the rulers they had removed. The girls were shipped in from all over. They had some things in common. All of them were beautiful, and they had honed their skills, they arrived the day before, so that they would be rested and ready to entertain by the time their clients arrived.

The two generals arrived by car, grateful it was four-wheel drive, as the road was no more than a track, and the snow lay thick and crisp. Their driver was competent though, and they felt safe. They arrived comfortable and ready to the promised rest and relaxation.

Inside the log cabin was warm and bright. Three beautiful women wore very little, and sat comfortably on the furniture. Two dark haired girls and one blonde.

The two men had enjoyed the company of these girls before and they all acknowledged each other. To say that they were friends was pushing it too far. The blonde stood up and poured drinks, passing a large brandy to each of the generals, smiling when she told them it would warm them up after the snow outside, and gave another one to each of the girls. Finally, she poured one for herself, and raised her glass in a toast to the men, wishing them an enjoyable weekend, and to the women, wishing them a profitable one. They all laughed and drank their drinks, each feeling the heat of the smooth spirit making its way down into their bellies. Where it sat. Not entirely alone.

The blonde smiled as they slumped into a gentle slumber. She hit the button on the phone, and listened.

The driver smoked his cigarette, leaning against the side of the car. This was an easy weekend for him, all he had to do was stay out of the way, and keep his mouth shut. He was a lucky guy. Right up until the silenced bullet took out the left side of his head.

The chopper landed just above the treeline, the two commandos who had taken out the driver took the two generals and the two sleeping girls to meet it, and loaded them in, strapping them in, and securing their handcuffs to the seats. The blonde in the ski suit climbed in and they lifted away from the snow, over the trees and over the border into NATO controlled territory.

The helipad was clear and ready when they landed. The commandos were replaced by others, and the still sleeping cargo, were loaded into a cargo plane, still handcuffed, and joined by the blonde. Together they flew through the cold night to land at RAF Northolt, where her employers were waiting. Their visitors were unloaded carefully, the girls still wrapped in the blankets she had found for them.

"Hello Katy." He wrapped his arms around her. "Another job, run to perfection. Nicely done." Her smile was softer than the one offered to the Generals. The truth was very simple. Whores and spies lived in the same world. Those that were good in both professions were able to control how they dealt with the world to make it work for them. In a country overrun by an occupying army, whores and spies were the most useful weapons that could be deployed.

When the girls woke up, they were paid what they were owed, and a substantial bonus, which they were glad to accept.

The Generals, however, were given some very stark choices. They could not go back. Their political overlords would not take kindly to their disappearance, or their pictures being released showing that they were in London. Their families would suffer. It would be an unhappy situation altogether. The alternative was to tell their new employers everything that they knew, and have a happy and safe retirement. There really was no choice.

They told their stories. Slowly at first, but in time they became fluent in their own traitorous way. The information they gave furthered the efforts of the men they had called their enemies. Their lives were not so terrible, they ate well, and lived in comfort, safer than they would have been. They could not contact their families, or friends, but that was the price they paid.

Giles left them with the men who were qualified and experienced in extracting the most from their guests and went back to work.

'Katy' went back to her home, and put the money she had earned into making the place she loved a viable possibility. The house and the land that surrounded it were the reason she did what she did, and the sanity in a mad world where she recovered from it.

43.

Halloween Party

The music was loud, she felt the beat from the pavement outside the house. Her breathing hitched, and she ran her hands over the sleek, smooth curves of the dress she was wearing. The black velvet hugged her body, and she smiled. This was her night. Halloween night was the best night of the year.

She rang the bell, and a girl opened the door, dressed as a witch. "Nice costume." She opened the door.

The thump of the music, the movement of the bodies, the heat of the dancing and the smell of the party filled her body. She pulled her coat around her body. She always felt the cold.

Slowly she moved through the hallway, where zombies and wizards danced. Slipping past them, she moved into another room, where the music was louder. A vampire moved in close, and twirled her through a turn. She smiled up into his face, and saw the panic in his eyes, when he looked into her eyes. Not for her. She was looking for something else.

The kitchen was filled with warm happy people, laughing, and eating. She checked out the food, but there was nothing there that she wanted. A sigh, a breath, left her body. Two pirates stood in the doorway. She remembered a pirate who had been fun. One of them wrapped an arm around her waist, and she leaned into him. His mouth reached down for hers. No. This was not what she was looking for. She smiled, and walked away.

Into another room, it was quieter there. The thump and bump of the beat was in the background. She shimmied through the crowd, and was back-to-back with a witch. Twice they moved their bodies together and away. For a moment, she considered the option. It was possible. No. It was the wrong choice. The girl turned towards her, and laughed, folding in for a hug. It was an interesting sensation but not the one she was looking for.

She spotted him. The one she had come here for. He was sitting, leaning against some cushions. The crowd was thick between them, but his eyes were locked with hers. She could have called him to her. She could have pulled him from his seat. But subtlety was maybe the better option.

Turning left and right, she moved slowly through the crowd to get to him. Until she was a step away. Until she could smell him, feel him, sense him. He stood up as she got to him.

"Hello." He stood over her. "You're a vampire. Which is really rather wonderful, because I am a vampire hunter." He stood apart from her, but his eyes burned into hers. His lips were inches from hers.

"Shall we dance?" She moved a step away from him, and smiled when he stepped towards her. Their bodies fitted together as she had known they would. His hands rested on her hips. The heat from his skin skittered through her skin, warming her. His lips grazed hers, and travelled down to her jaw, and then her neck. This was the one she had been searching for. His warmth filled her. "Come with me?" His eyebrow lifted, but he let her take his hand.

They walked through the party, and out into the darkness. The woods across the road called. Her hand in his, his other hand on her hip. Her smile calling him on. Their steps halted at the side of the lake. His kiss, as she leaned back against the trunk of a tree, fizzing through her body.

"Funny thing." He whispered into her neck. "I know this is not just a costume. I know this is you." Her kiss, on his tender neck, smelling of fresh soap and blood faltered. "My costume isn't just a costume either." He rested the stake against her rib cage.

"Come with me. For ever." She leaned hard into him and the stake. Her breath came in short rasps. "Let me take you with me, we can fly away, and we will be like this forever. Trust me, or don't. Your choice." Her eyes opened wide, and held his.

Her lips, her tongue, on his neck, the scent of his jugular driving her wild. She checked his eyes. Her hands wrapped around his. "Your choice. I know what I want." He groaned, letting go of the stake. Her lips drew back, her teeth sinking into his neck, feeding the animal he craved. His body rose and fell with hers. The moon hung high over the lake, and the distant thump of the music from the party played for them as they flew away, lifting over the lake, he would be hers forever.

Finally, after years of searching, he was hers, and she was his. They had centuries to work out the rest of the details.

44.

Naredon Hall

The boots were in their box, where she knew they would be. She had worn them the first day she had seen Naredon Hall, she had been young, newly married and very much in love. Her husband had brought her home, after a quiet wedding, and a few months in London and she had been entirely intimidated by the house, and everyone in it. Her boots were cream coloured and laced up as tight as the corset which was supposed to hide the growing bump she carried.

His Mother, the Dowager met her with more frost than a January morning, enquiring as to her health and whether she was likely to enjoy the country, after her busy life in the theatre. The staff, and there were still a crowd of them then, were polite and deferential, but she could hear the sneer in their voices. They were right, he had married beneath him, she was definitely not worthy of the house or the life, but she loved him with all her heart, and she knew he loved her. It would have to be enough.

When the baby arrived, and they realized she would not be going anywhere, and that she had done the duty of an aristocrat's wife, and provided an heir, the frost melted a little. She threw herself into the house and gardens, learning everything there was to know with joy and gales of laughter, she was an actress after all. She began to win them around. The second baby, a sweet pink cheeked girl sealed the deal. She was as accepted as she was going to be.

He still took her breath away. His handsome face, and his gentle heart warmed her every day, and his love kept her safe from the world. Three years of wonder and bliss in a house which had been built eight hundred years before, and had seen the changes that time brings, came to an abrupt end when he returned home with a piece of paper that he had signed to volunteer for the war that had just begun. He was excited, and she had to admit, despite her worries for him and her fear at being left alone, that he looked very handsome in his uniform. He was among the first very brave souls to sign up, and he kissed her goodbye, promising that it would all be over by Christmas, and they would have such a jolly time, when he came home. 1914 was a year when a great many women, in houses grand and small, kissed goodbye the men they loved and waited, patiently for their return.

He was right, he did come home, on leave before they shipped him off to France, where he would write her sad, desperate letters, from the mud and the cold, trying to sound jolly and hopeful in a joyless and hopeless place, and missing by a mile. She would cry and send him her love and stories of home.

Three years later the letters were still coming, but less often, and the hope for a resolution was gone entirely. Most of the men who had worked in the gardens and the house had gone to join him, and they were a house full of women, trying hard to raise her children, and run the huge place.

When a letter came from the Colonel of his battalion, she was unsurprised, so many had been lost. She had locked the devastation into her heart and gone to find her mother-in-law. They wept together, and gently told the children that their father would not come home. Not for Christmas. Not ever. A few years had passed since that dreadful night, when she had wandered the halls like a wraith in the moonlight.

The government had asked her to pay almost every bit of cash that they had, and she had handed it over. She shed no tears for money, but understood why so many of her husband's contemporaries had married rich Americans, instead of an actress who made church mice look well off.

She spent a great deal of time, when she was free from volunteering in the hospital that most of her home had become, remembering the time she had shared with him, before everything was about the war, and injuries and death. Most particularly, she remembered the hotels where they had stayed. She had felt so well looked after. The stories her mother-in-law told her of visitors to the house back in the glory days, of royalty, and every local Lord and Lady were similar. They had been cared for and cossetted too.

Over the course of a bad winter followed by a wet spring when the crops needed sunshine, followed by more rain and finally some sunshine, the farm produced very little income. The chickens, thank the Lord, gave them eggs which they could eat and sell, and the woodlands gave timber to keep the fires blazing. They were better off than many.

The idea started from that tiny seed, and grew, as the hospital emptied, out into the world, or into the cemeteries, she began to plan the future, when she would need to make money to provide for her children, and keep the house safe for her son to inherit. Those men who returned from the war and wanted to go back into service came back to the hall, many did not return at all, and some of those who did, wanted a different life.

On the day that she told them her plan, some of them were scandalized. The idea seemed to go against everything that they had been taught to believe.

"I know it is a complete change. However, I have also heard stories about royalty who rested their heads here, and friends, families, huge parties. It is no different, except that they will be contributing to the upkeep of this wonderful house, and all of us. The work will be much the same, but we will be giving them the chance to spend time here, in a place that we all love. We will be giving them a dream that they can carry for the rest of their lives. We will be sharing Naredon Hall." She watched while they thought about it. There were a few who would not accept the changes, and gave notice. She accepted their decision with as much graciousness as she could muster.

Then it was full steam ahead with the changes. She had to give up the family rooms to the guests who may or may not arrive, and they had all moved to more cramped quarters, but it was done. The doors would open on Naredon Hall Hotel for the first time, and she would wear her boots.

The leather creaked as she forced her foot inside. Everything else had changed around her, but the boots had remained the same as the day she wore them to come to a new home and a new life.

Three couples, all American were expected before long and she checked her reflection in the glass, before taking herself on a tour, to the kitchen, where the cooks were working hard, and to the dining room, which was laid with beautiful silver and crystal, through the bedrooms which were cleaned and beautifully prepared and finally to the reception area in the front hall where the young man who has been a footman was now sitting calmly behind the desk in the main hall. He jumped to his feet when he saw her, but sank back to his seat when she waved his polite gesture away.

The Dowager had stayed away, but not this time from distrust or hauteur. She had wished her daughter in law luck, kissed her on the cheek, and told her that her son had been a lucky man to have found her. There had been tears shed, and a great deal of nose blowing before the dignified old lady had told her that she planned to stay out of the way on the following day.

The bell at the front door rang, and the tiny upstairs maid, picture perfect in her black dress and white apron walked calmly to open it. She dipped a curtsey to the new arrivals.

"Good afternoon, Sir, Madam. Welcome to Naredon Hall." Her smile was wide, but not as wide as that of the visitors.

45.

Thank you, and goodnight

To those of you who have been with me from the start of this journey, I am so grateful. To those of you who have jumped on board recently, welcome, where have you been?

I hope you liked the short stories. I really do. You have no idea how much time and hope has gone into these.

Just so that you know there will be a new novel out soon. If you haven't read my novels yet, please do! There are more on the way!

I said at the start of this collection that my family have put up with me being distracted, and it's true, they have. They have also given me endless support, belief and joy, for which I am beyond grateful, and of which I am entirely undeserving.

Thank you. Thank you. Thank you. Can't say it enough.

Printed in Great Britain
by Amazon